Collected Poems

Collected Poems

by MAUREEN DUFFY

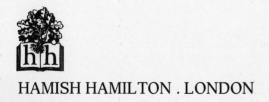

HAMISH HAMILTON . LONDON

This collection first published in Great Britain 1985
by Hamish Hamilton Ltd
Garden House 57-59 Long Acre London WC2E 9JZ

British Library Cataloguing in Publication Data

Duffy, Maureen
    Collected poems.
    I. Title
    821'.914   PR6054.U4

    ISBN 0-241-11595-7
    ISBN 0-241-11667-8 Pbk

Typeset by Pioneer, East Sussex
Printed in Great Britain by
St. Edmundsbury Press

Contents

EARLY POEMS 1949—66

LYRICS FOR THE DOG HOUR

THE VENUS TOUCH

EVESONG

MEMORIALS OF THE QUICK AND THE DEAD

THE GARLAND

'I am certain of nothing but the holiness of the heart's affections . . .'

John Keats

Preface

These poems have been written over the space of thirty-five years and therefore a list of the many journals and magazines in which they first appeared would be impossibly cumbersome. To all of them I owe my thanks but I should particularly like to acknowledge my debt to the publishers of my earlier collections: to Hutchinsons for *Lyrics For The Doghour,* to Weidenfeld and Nicolson for *The Venus Touch;* to Sappho Publications for *Evesong* and to Hamish Hamilton for *Memorials of The Quick and The Dead.*

M.D.
London, 1985

EARLY POEMS 1949—66

Rapunzel

I came to her tower in the evening
With the trembling breath of darkness
Soft upon my cheek. The long bright ladder
Of her hair she tumbled to my feet.

I climbed —
Hand over hand caught in its silken mesh.
She fretful would not listen
She would go out — and pouted
I cut the golden plait and made it fast

Then down we slipped leaving the tiny room
To its whispers and dim corners.
She ran before me on quicksilver feet
In the youth of the year
When the eager surge of springing life
Beat in the earth
Charging the lips of leaf on leaf and blade on blade
With quick response
Thrusting the quivering branches upward in urgent strength

So we came to dim-lit streets
Then the gay laughter of an Easter fair
Blazing beside still water
Bright with a hundred flares
Shrill with a million voices.

She laughed and pulled me by the hand
We ran and played —
Wave upon wave of pressing shapes
Hot breath and clamorous sound
Beat about us.

We were flung dazed and panting
On the cool moist ground.
I loved her then and had her close
Bright-haired, large eyed
Yet I loosed her as she wished
She ran before me on quicksilver feet
And was drowned in the flood of the fair.

A thousand years is a long time to sing alone
With only the persistent echo of a song
Beating back from the blank walls
In the hush of a passing age.

Impromptu Verses on a Tutor Removing into Whitechapel

Wakes in Whitechapel now Miss Taylor,
    Attunes her academic mind
To hear above the rising city
    The call to labours unrefined.

She contemplates her prints and volumes
    Just arbiter of 'The Sublime',
While down below her early neighbours
    Lift up their hearts to get the time.

The eye picks out an orange cover,
    Orwell reposes on the shelf
Approving in a cheap edition
    This means to economic health.

And from her walls among the moderns
    Etched like a modest epitaph,
The Cambridge backs survey benignly
    Miss Taylor languid in the bath.

Lapped round by tides of wit and wisdom
    More rare than Minton, Sèvres or Spode,
Blooming, a cultural oasis,
    In deserts of the Mile End Road.

Ulysses

Now Ulysses tacking the lean tides of his age
Skirting remembered shores where rocks snarl black,
His swart mind swinging in a rusty cage,
And cargo of traveller's tales with sea-salt smack,
Strides on the quayside the windy decks of life,
Loud with the unfleshed mouths of those he fought.
His warped eyes cringe at sun-strike from a sailor's knife,
Or chime of sudden steel his coiled ear caught.
He dare not turn to Menelaus' shore
Where mumbling Helen wrinkled as a fig,
Stirs in the moany draught about the door
And scrapes a withered toe against her leg,
But plots an uneasy course under the skull's high dome
Among the subtle shoals that shape his island home.

Young Child

Half table height lucky in love you wander
Beginning to be, yourself uncharted land.
Voyage in your own country traveller
At home in paths we cannot understand.
This kingdom of your heart each day uncover,
Head high in sun, flower bright as summer birds —
Time that memory cannot recover
Vanished or ever you come to words.

O you will be strong a Prince to conquer the earth,
And lord of the moon when we have crumbled to dust,
But always the child you are will haunt your days,
Boy you set out to find in your morning birth,
The only man in the world you dare not trust,
Alone with yourself walking the world's ways.

For Maria Assuntina

Mamma I can never call by name,
Mother by luck and love, my tongue holds back
And cannot form caresses from my shame.
In your far country cicala in a black
Night rubs out a wounded love song in the grass,
Hot stars burn in a charcoal sky, I know
The breeze is tender in your mountain pass.
Here in slum streets the chill winds blow,
Your life unfurls in damp curls, swift hands set
Beauty to grace an evening at the bar,
'D'you like my new hair do?'
Your lame tongue trips on unaccustomed words yet
Smiling you say what halt speech cannot mar,
'If you are good God may be good to you.'

An Irish Poet for His Country

You have played my puppeteer too long
Danced me in love and through the hungry dark
Quickening to every sentimental song.
Hanrahan who rose like a tipsy lark
To sing in your second dawn with his rioting tongue
Who shaped my youth, is fifteen years now stark
In his grave, and still his tune runs on
Clear as deep waters where the swans embark.

I know your mockeries, indignant shadows
Darken your whitewashed walls like a hanging man.
I know your strings have a thin untunable sound
Like the difficult breath that rasps through an old man's nose,
Betrayal of credulous blood that leapt and ran —
And yet I return to dance to the fiddles' round.

Heroes

On the Death of a Labour Leader

Sickness can show us who our heroes are.
Robin lies bleeding, all his wounds unbound;
Calling his name his friend runs through the town,
Runs up the stair, breaks down the door,

Takes in his arms the man whose power
Cleft willow wands and put the law to shame.
The hero dies and with him all the band,
The carefree life, the green enchanted hour —

Long forest days, good fighting, comradeship;
Reading the tale we weep to see the image fade.
So he lies now, whose arrow tongue made
Slender arguments like willow wands to split,

Called up the brave boys when the rich men passed
Riding their privilege through the coal-black streets,
Took their gold coins of power to feed the poor, freed
Prisoners cramped lifelong in chains of class.

There in the narrow bed our image lies —
Kier Hardy, Sidney Street, the dole —
Emblems of conflicts never learnt in school
That bred a brotherhood the wise

Children lapped in success will never know.
Oh send our faith striding the streets;
Tie up his heart's wounds that we may hear
His challenge sound again and we shall go.

Friday Night

Old Charlie flighting darts peers through the smoke,
Aims for the bull, turns, sups and smacks blue lips,
    Cuffs off the handy scum.
    With mock eyes then, appraises
    Young Tom's drink giddy shots
        Wild of the board.

And sixty years, sober and drunk about,
Sweat half dry, dreg down to weekend wisdom
    How to speed an arrow
    Through thick air; and the boy,
    Bum-tight trousers shape him
        Like a young girl.

These two then, wrapt one in their bitter cloak
To keep the world at bay, invisible,
    Play their fierce game of dreams.
    Talk drifts about them as
    They chalk the ghost figures
        And never speak.

Time calls across the bar into the dark,
The lights go down, goodnight knocks at the heart.
    Idly the damp cloth scrubs
    The magic numbers out.
    Bang the swing door; don't cry
        Who won or lost.

In The Gardens

Picking a delicate way among rose and willow
Miss Allardyce in the gardens
Has come to fashion languid stitches
In the gentle afternoon,
Watches with startled eyes the endless come and go,
Chooses a solitary pool of sunlight
To place her chair,
Reclines her braided head with almost sensual grace.

As leaves in drought fall,
Leisurely air-ambling fall,
So pass her days.
Digs no grave, uprears no monument,
Keeps three cats and is at ease.

Child in the gardens,
Transmuted, transcending,
Become wave of the water,
Grew among the grass,
Found a unicorn with golden hooves
Among the trees,
Coaxed it, out into the sunlight,
Fed it on fragrance of a broken flower,
Lost it among the reeds by the water —
And smudged his face with crying.

She did not stir.

This young man wrote verses once.
Now turned critic,
Has three more years of reputation
And comes to sleep on the littered grass.

She is unaware.

The elderly clergyman with the stiff hands
Will die in the spring,
When canaries sing in back streets, and green comes.
He is worried for his wife with the faded smile
And for his people —

Yet there remains winter.
And there is still time,
Still time for the sun.
He trusted.
Let him never be confounded.

But she does not hear.

There are two lovers by the water
Whose yesterday are joined
And hands like birds restless-winged:
'O had she speaking eyes to break my pain.'
Trapped in her own unspoken words —
'O if he loved he would not ask for words.'
They never know that all their doubts are hopes,
And all their love a questioning.

Miss Allardyce in the gardens
Impartial, unaware,
Untouched by human loves that lap about her shores,
She has her tranquil joys,
Trembles a little in the evening air.
World within world she rises,
Leaves nothing of herself that shall disturb,
Only her shadow wistful at her heels —
That, too, shall vanish with her falling sun.

Girls Learning

A lick of paint rims their scrubbed sullen mouths,
      Girls pout in mirrors, gossip,
      Hum blue notes, their selves laid by
      Go meek to morning worship.
Last night they trembled when the rough boys' cry
      Strummed their taught nerve strings in the park,
And kissed their hard mouths in the hugging dark.

They turn the page hearing of Juliet
      She and her bright boy who lost.
      Their thoughts fly up, brush the pane
      Opaque with dust; chalk motes tossed
In a thin shaft of sun silt the dull brain.
      Only the golden hero
Pictured in the desk, burns with a sullen glow.

Warm Spring winds sighing lay their bodies wide
      Tranced in the pale sun they lounge,
      Hearing the younger children
      Chanting as they skip. They scrounge
 A morsel of rich scandal, awaken
      With the bell that bears them back
To the dull wisdom of the printed book.

Unsure, eager, they go to meet their boys,
      Flash, sauntering careless, sparring
      Loud to hide uncertainty.
      Quick to outbid in daring
Scared of the tides that flush them through, they try
      To kiss half questions in their dark —
Learning each other, or themselves, there in the park.

A Woman's World

It is a woman's world from nine to five.
Bundled in old coats which obscure their sex,
Useless by day, put on with evening meals,
They shop for scandal, every tale believe;
    A toddler at their heels
Bribed with a biscuit to stand still for goodness sake,
Whimpers with boredom, tries to vex

Into attention, draw them from the charm
Of sickness, married war or pound of flesh.
Prams give them status, block pavements with their pride,
So too the round belly, face madonna calm.
    Like ships against the tide
They roll a little, both feet anchored firm, thrown back,
To brace the weight. Their lives, a mesh

Of tiny incident, entrap and bind
Them. London's a world away where husbands act
A mystic ritual of grave affairs.
Seeking a romance they'd never dare to find,
    A magazine dream theirs
Indulged in afternoons beside a damped down fire,
They wait the coming of the mastering fact.

My Sisters the Whores

My sisters the whores, out for love or money,
    In Magdalen midnight
    Parade the Circus ring;
Their lips paint purple under neon lights
Are yours, at a price, for kissing.
Rampant as robins on a boundary wall,
They guard their trading terrain against all.

Like other costers they supply a need,
    The lure of bargains
    Hunted on the sly.
Their wares displayed under the smoky rain,
Tantalizing the bright fruits piled high,
Rotten when tasted, quickly flung away,
Uneasily forgotten in the sober day.

Last customers drain down the tube. Silence
    Stamps out the butt-end
    Of the night. Homewards
They drift, peel off their clothes, borrow or lend
Face cream or hair pins, count up the night's rewards.
After the harsh male handling of their charms
They find soft comfort in each other's arms.

Though I for virtue's sake, or fear, lie still alone,
    My hand is empty, hides no stone.

Women four

Sappho was mistress of a singing school.
These riddle the three Rs; their skins grown grey
With fossilizing chalk. Days run to rule,
Love is an outcast, beauty hides away
Behind a gym-slip or a manly tie.
Girls grow to mock their eccentricities.

They queue at morning break for tepid tea
Soothing their throats parched in a desert of words,
Angry at fancied slights they see
In every childish laugh, like stopping birds
Robbed of prey they turn to rend each other,
Haggle for armchairs by the radiator.

Each month when longing moves them blurred eyes stray
Over the slim legs making patterns
Of white on green, pure in an abstract way,
Notice a child's soft nape whisped with light down,
But the soiled collar, trace of grime,
Restores a perilous equilibrium.

Dedicated; at fifty the walls close in,
Long corridors stand insolently on end.
'Suffering from a grave attack of sin,
A rest is needed,' perhaps a term will mend
Years of fulfilment in a vocation,
Ease the fierce agony of a martyr's crown.

Retired among cats, visits from old girls,
The garden, time to enjoy your pension,
Music, forty years of culture prized like pearls
From oyster books; one day the milkman
Finds yesterday's half-pint still patient at the door.
'A plus' for effort, public service: close the score.

Women six

They dance together since the lads are shy,
  Scarcely touching breast to soft breast
    But hand to hand, drawn close
Or thrust away as drums dictate. Their eyes
      Set upon space,
Indifferent to the boys who burn in the shadows,

They rock, half turn in a mindless trance,
  Part animal, part frenzy
    Of the god, lithe lust
Who hunted Agave; a sudden glance,
      The bold eyes cast
Modestly low, lessons learnt from tuppeny novelettes.

The record ends, the golden voice sinks down,
  They join their partners brash with beer,
    Giggle, pat hair, sip gin
Or bitter lemon; the thin boy acts the clown,
      Wildly tries to win
Them from the magic box. A disc begins to spin,

Without a word they move away, summoned
  By song. Boy in the brown suit
    Dare-all drunker than his mates,
Leans his head on the tall girl's shoulder, stunned
      By her swift grace,
And still she dances on, no stir ruffles her face.

The throbbing jukebox throws a green glow around
Through which the figures swim like eels
    In smoky seas. Afire
To break the flowing spell of sound
    Douse his desire
With lips and eyes, a gipsy boy, gold ring in one ear,

Pinches and slaps them as they pass. At once
    A scream, a broken glass, blood runs,
        The rite is shattered.
Bewildered the boy escapes the hunt.
            Music is heard;
Blank-eyed the girls return, bound by the singing word.

The god has power still
That holds them dancing to his will.

For George Lamming

Though dumb as dirt two centuries now slavey
You hold up black paws, palms pink as ham,
Show stripe, chain chafe, blood spilled as cheap as gravy,
Nigger boy, coloured, you there Big Sam,
Call darkness as a witness of your wrong,
Yet every Mick, Wop, Jew-boy has them too,
Brands of the underdog, bars of the captive's song;
There's no monopoly of suffering for you.

Your mother sweated long hours in the sun
For cane to sweeten others', whitemen's cups;
Mine's paleface swam long hours in the dark,
Drowned in the swirling mists of starch, to turn
White sugar into almond whirls, comfits, sweet sups
To fatten those men's wives. We bear the self-same mark.

Sparrows

Sparrows in the pecked-clean, wind-whip branches,
Clever — dicks of fluff, eating the parkey
Crusts of charity, puffing up small brown paunches,
Habitat the smoke, care nothing for the holy
Economic laws of smooth-skinned humanity;
Dig not no nor delve for leather jacket,
Wire worm to prove their basic utility;
Mess up the pavements; deafen with small-time racket;

Screech and claw, bossy, black-bibbed and tuckered;
Serenade no sunrise but cheap, cheap their pop song
From the ridge poles or the gorbals of the eaves.
Surely like saints and madman they are fathered.
Caught in the steel cat claws of our wrong
An eye marks their fall, and something in us grieves.

To Stanley Spencer

Live, walking where I've seen the dead arise,
In Cookham churchyard just before the bridge,
Shrug off tweed coats of grass, under wide skies
Dazzled with common sunlight, in a mild surprise
Smooth rumpled clothes and comb each other's hair
Tidy for judgement, I hear the chill knock,
Knock of busy hammers at their work. There
On the village dust tip, mouth full of nails to spare

Two red-capped men are crucifying Christ
And humming as they drive the murder home.
Call the cool visitors to come and stare:
I won his warm brown jacket when we diced,
I feel the metal jarring on the bone,
And doomsday calls reveille at my ear.

Oxford, 31 May 1958

17

To E. B.

Cecco called Dante his master and a fool;
Canzoni they wrote each other, sonnets
Flew, shuttlecocks of criticism back and forth,
Verona to Provence. If we communicate
It is by notes exchanged like wicked children
Underneath the breath or business wise
'Enclosed please find . . .' The posts are faster
But we lack the ties that bound those ballad boys,
Exiled and scattered through the world.
'A common culture' so the text books say.
They spat and joked and told their dreams,
Pitted their girls against each others' charms,
A culture common as the clay.

Going Like A Man

I walk as working men walk,
A little stiff, weight thrown back on the heels,
Drunk from the punishment of the last round,
Eight to five, hands in the pockets,
Head sunk against the wind,
Coat tails aswing, heavy with dust and age;
Yer working coat.

At least it used to be so I remember
When I met him in the November dark,
Last out through the high iron gate,
Breath drawing cautious and shallow
Through the pinched nostrils; gassed of course
Fifty years ago, gulped, groped blind
And will die gasping, holding the green slime
In his mouth

Waiting for a polite moment to spit.
We strolled slowly, me tuning my quick steps
To his tired jaunt, a taste of fog
Rancid on the tongue, his eyes kohl rimmed,
Clinkered, back-chatting home to tea.
The works are closed now. Six months retired
He mourned the coffin of their trade to the town hall.
Not much of a job

But it had sheltered them through the thirties.
They were too old to change: one picks up glasses,
Some sun themselves on the old men's corner,
He ekes out with assistance and can always
Lend me a quid. I borrow it out of pride,
His and mine. Rich in polemic still,
As we match steps pint for pint,
The fine hands

Grow flowers of memory out of the smoke.
I wonder sometimes if anyone understands
Even these words we use anymore. Curious now
As stranded whales or the old Coffee Pot
Plying the single track of the transport museum,
They were monolithic as steam engines;
We are flash tin cans on pram wheels beside;
I prefer to walk.

And I can't get it out of my blood that step,
Go swinging along still as if in company,
All jaunting tired together like the dead
In Burghclere chapel their crosses heaped for burning,
Toys tidily put away, and strolling into eternity.
Passers-by stare as I go, wondering where
And why, whether there's room for that gait
On the moon.

I wonder too but can't ask him.
'We're beyond all that now,' his wife says.
'No concern of ours. We did our best,
Inched forward a little. You pick up
Where we left off. Why should we fret anymore?'
I watch him upturn the hassock geranium leaves,
Earthy under the pinching finger and thumb,
Budding drops of thin blood.

Always last out after the home-flowing tide
Of men in step. How do they journey now?
My muscles have learnt a kind of conformity
That takes me through November darks,
The rancid streets of railway cottages
Standing back, lit windows peering through thick lashes
Of store curtain, under an occasional lamp,
Walking in company.

For a Nameless Child

Rare piece of human, bundle of desires,
Or call you pet names, curse or croon asleep,
Whatever falls most easy to the tongue, deep
Among drifts of dreams your small self stirs,
No name to call it out into the light;
Ease you who shall be from your swaddling bands,
Limbo of moulding womb; unclench small hands
Imprisoning selfhood in their tiny might.

So here I make this rhyme to set you free
And charm your childhood with a witch's art;
Baptize and name you in this simple rite;
Exorcize evils with my magic key.
Then take this christening gift spelled from the heart;
Harm keep away, she has her name tonight.

LYRICS FOR THE DOG HOUR

Missa Humana

Kyrie

Where were you when the child cried
With tongue of fire in the cinder skull
Where were you?

Who heeds them, their brown twig limbs
Crossed on the empty sack of flesh
Who heeds them?

What moves you, only your own pain
Death at your door, your face in the glass
What moves you?

Gloria

Dust glitters; sweepings of sky
Recreate, fuse in fresh worlds.
The suns decline and cool, the paling dwarfs go out
Rewake to elements that seed new stars.

In the tides of our flesh
Brief cells rise and set
In a resistless dying to beget
Bone, blood and brain.

Children of the mind cities rise,
Patched and piecemeal we cloak the earth
With art, erect talismen
Of note and line and word on word;

Mark snow crystal, corolla
Damasked, enamelled;
Herring-bone of leaf; the tendons
That flex birdclaw and finger;

And dying swansong of what was forever
Is and shall be among starshine and birdcall,
That shall put out the dark.

Credo

Belief hangs laggard.
Words rustle husk dry, confound
With statement, half truth.
We wear them as masks
Over the subtle coil of our hearts.
Dare we affirm or deny,
Contraries answer us back,
The rational smile justifying the knife,
Lips that close on a threat.

Somewhere the truth skulks afraid,
Sleeps at night a curled child in the attic
Where we bring it food,
The nurture of dreams,
Creeping stealthy through the sleeping house.

Oh will it ever be strong,
Grown tall enough to stride downstairs
Out into the white stare of the world;
Walk upright, unchallenged through the wide fields?

Pater Noster

Crust, crumb, grains in the palm of the hand
Be manna for us, feed.
Ant men we toil, furrow,
Unfurl steel banners furnace red,
Beggar our neighbour,
Climb upward on his bent head.
We have done and do and will be done to
A roundabout of ills bred
Of the wheel we are warped to
That we turn
And turning bleed.

Sanctus

As the folding of wings,
The sigh of steam at day's end,
Feet home-going through the gates,
Eased at last from day's clang and press,
Downhill now
As a bird doves down
Homing over twilight fields
Peace falls on streets
Feathered with dusk.

Tomorrow wakes to shoals of light.

Benedictus

Look we have broken time.
The pendulum is down
That swung us between past and future.

Now there is only now;
Held between our eyes like love
The minutes bloom poignant as roses.

Now time is space shrunk to a hand's breadth
Who can divide us from each other
Or resurrect the tyranny of difference?

Among the relative stars
Men walk familiar as Adam
Gardened in Eden.

Agnus Dei

Oh I speak out now, I answer
Myriad voiced. Hydra head I am,
Herd I feed, lift my sheep's face,
Baa pitiful, dogged and shepherded,
Sleek meat for butcher's knife.

Come to the shambles you shall see
Me there hang my head,
Throat slit from ear to ear.
Brothers in blood my eyes pop,
As they did in life, in fear.

Despise me if you dare.
Cut your milk teeth on my soft ribs;
The sweetest flesh laps bone.
Feed as I have on grass
Whose every tear winces the supple blades.

All die and dying succour
Unless we break this round of flesh on flesh
And feed on air.
We lift our flocked snouts blunt.
Who calls us here?

Amen

In the end then there is no end.
Voices of children call from the dark,
Fleshed in the womb eyes kindle,
Seed seeks its narrow road to life;
In the end there is no end.

Though we twist and torture awry
The shoot grows straight for the sun,
Out of fermenting clay green foam quickens,
Leaves froth from the breaking boughs
Though we twist and torture awry.

In the end there is only beginning.
The petals of light scattered
On the dark inflame new fires
We blow to torch us with our dying breath.
Lit by our own stars we burn and in the end there is no end.

A Dublin Diary

Bailey's

Humped under rainstrike,
My name unknown —
Among the fifty most common in all the land —
Treading hasty in other men's steps,
Wet Bloomsway, the pavement grey,
Now I settle for this
To pass til boat time, home time
With ringing of glasses;
A few bob in my pocket,
Spent up on sedative stout,
Saffron smoked cod and chips
Gulped afoot by the straight river bank
Where nothing's changed
Though houses are gone,
Busses have run down trams,
And skirts no longer drag in the dirt
As the prints on the wall tell me they did.
Joyce's mask gleams beside them,
The smile caught on the corners of the mouth.

Sandycove

And I understand now why men buy towers,
Buy or build it's all the same,
Wanting to set round and solid
In themselves, with water and sky
Their backdrop and the small people
Staring up at their walls.
Making themselves towers,
Drawn taut in a circle against the enemy
With no keystone cornering
For foothold,
The separate blocks morticed,
And the door high.
Thirty years set stone on stone,
Thoughts hewn, hacked to fit,
I've built
Til now I stand
Against backdrop of water and sky,
Letting the little folk pass
Though the walls weep in the winter
And a round room pinches the pocket
For eating and sleeping and song.

Folk Song

As I roved out through Dublin town,
The gentle speech fell all around;
No hearts were pierced, no faces wet
For present men.

They hang their rebels from the trees,
The tattered rags shake in the breeze,
Their flesh long crumpled down to dust
Silts up the will.

The pretty girl on the telly screen
Ran fingers up and down the theme;
Harped, 'Lay me lovely Johnny do,'
With smile awry.

For Johnny's young and Johnny's gay
And always looks the other way.
His only lust's a thick blonde head
In every glass.

Fill he me rue the maiden's cry,
I'll catch a husband by and by;
Across the ocean seek I will
An eager man.

And though he doesn't mind the priest
He'll mind my body at the least,
And that is more than many do
In Dublin town.

A Song Unheard

What happened to you then Willy,
'Foolish passionate man,'
Pressed in the collected edition
There at the back of the shelf?

My mind was a white bird wheeling
High over a land run blood.
I would not humour their weakness
Nor pamper their harlot whim.
What I wrote was sung to all men
Not to Paudeen alone.
My words sink into their hearts like stone.

Travelling Second

Have compassion on the dumb ox,
Cattle shipped forward on the hoof
Under the heel of the first-class passengers,
Or aft, rug-headed on two legs, steerage,
Sick all nights, slumped in the gangways,
Going East for work; my boy Paddy
Cut down to size in father's cast-offs.
A family dozen all told, faces half formed
In the featureless flesh, stray humanity.

I sleep on deck under Jupiter,
Clean and cold, wrapped in a borrowed coat.

The bullocks are first ashore,
A-canter, slipping to their knees
On the wet planking and goaded up
Over the bridge into darkness,
Lowing sadly. The others
Pick up cases and stand, heads drooping,
Patient, for officialdom to come on duty,
Admit them into the grey city morning.
They turn their faces towards the gangway,
Murmuring quietly.

Lyrics for the dog hour

I

One

When it fell they were busy with other things.
One looked up first, blinded, seared,
Cried flame.
The other running to see took fire,
Charred in an instant into residual ash,
Rose, phoenixed. Now self consuming
Fans its own embered flesh.

Let yours sink down; I blaze enough to scorch the dark.

Two

Five a.m. is the dog hour, small hour.
I wake to grey washes of light against the pane.
The dustmen will come at seven clanging the bins.
A cat screams into the dawn echoing my lust.
Soon the suburban gossip of birds: nesting and young.
I turn on my belly, arms pierced with cramp.
So she would lie under me. My mouth seeks the pillow,
Adrenalin runs in the veins, green acid
Corroding the gut. I have drawn imaginary cords
About her throat but they were only grass.

Three

When I am with her the eyes say, 'Love me.'
Can the eyes lie?

Apart, the fingers of doubt prise up the lid of her heart.
Inside the smooth tick

Oiled by custom, reassuring; all's well about
Til I ring, demand

Answers, questions: a hiccupping insistence,
Mechanical voice

Sounding retreat. I would try to walk soft
But bedded flames

Run wildfire through the bone.

Four

I am become greedy for her
Overnight. Eyes finger the shadows
Sketch the slit belly
Charcoal on grey
Remembering the hallowed throat
The quick cold vein my teeth
Would have savaged.
I will be gentle,
Gentle you into rose.
Colours are born of the sun.

Five

Down the highway sailor,
The one you picked up,
Sea-legs home proud of his tattered sail.
Ships again in his head
Seas, breakers of words,
Half-remembered rocks he foundered on.
Wrecked ashore he moons about the docks
Kicking an aimless day,
Tacking from course to course.
The painted image plunges and beckons.
Let him be gone again,
Chance maelstrom and drift,
Into the hurl of your deep.

II

One

Peacocking among pigeons
Blue woman, a jewelled dagger in her hand,
Queens it through travellers,
The to-and-fro of journeys, packs, luggage,
The shout of porters,
Aurioled with dusty sunlight.

Trains call away.
Eyes are full of distance:
Lines beckon to time's edge.
Already the commonplace is out of mind;
Seas, deserts replace with infinity.

But I am going further than any of them.
She is waiting for me.

Two

Laughter we weren't prepared for
Came suddenly a shower
Of light notes falling,
Caught us without cover;
Drenched,
Our eyes held.
Now the more common lightning
Strikes us through.

Three

Today the moon says no.
Taboos bind, teach me a patience,
A lingering after better than the quick kill,
Death.
I visit the soft flesh
With kisses only.
Hands that would ravage,
Caress.
Let my hunter's cunning grow
With the waxing moon
To consummation come
And my touch tear cries from the white throat.

III

Truce calls, the trumpets sound,
Back I crawl to lick wounds.
A skirmish only: no honour gained,
Nothing lost perhaps
But I count armour, weapons.
Tomorrow will call me to front line again.
Now I duck beneath trench tops,
Brew tea, boast of bouts before.

At dawn a whistle.
I rub sleep from my eyes,
Stagger into a grey light.
You are still asleep.
I look across to where you lie
So close I could reach a hand,
A thought's flight.

Last night enemy-friend
You cratered me,
Met me more than half-way,
Held pistol to my head,
No quarter.
Somehow I stumbled away,
Maimed, half-blind.

I warm my hands stretched to a blaze,
Among friends, waiting
For the whistle to sound again;
And we renew our love
Under the whine of the guns.

IV

Poor poems you are drunk with me.
The voices pour into my ears,
Features revolve. There's a woman
I could love
But chink, chink, the bitter glasses.
She has a touch, only a touch;
Something about the eyes,
Or is it the mouth?
I look more closely.
Features dissolve. Your eyes mock
Out of hers.
The mind staggers, overturns tables.
I know you are sitting at home.
If I could be there
No images would torment
With dancing fantasy.

V

I hoard up now against our winter,
Pack in the black hole of my heart
And stamp down hard,
Words, looks to nourish
When I stir in the long sleep
Troubled by dreams
And all is bitter outside.

Enemies take, friends give hostages.
Take mine: a picture, a brass heart
You make shiver with a touch,
A spinning disc that lets fall
My anguish by proxy in a summer afternoon,
The seasons are confounded.
Dust powders the leaves beyond the window
And snows drifts in the cavern where I lie.

Let them plead for me,
Wolves' prey in a devouring time,
That I wake to sunlight
And autumn may be Spring.

VI

Bialacoil

Last come, travel tired, soiled,
I push the door in.
The agent smiles, shows me the multi-coloured map;
Lots taken, parcelled out,
The rich land gone long since,
Seed cropped and pasture booked,
Foursquare settlements grounded,
A town with bank, an opera house.
I turn away.

'One moment, friend,'
He points beyond the suburbs.
'Here's a bit nobody fancied,
Overlooked. Needs hard work,
Clearing dead boughs and scrub.
Come, I'll show you.'

Beyond the last house we climb the hill.
A noonday silence.
Brown rocks jut dragon's teeth
From the yielding soil.
'This place, what you can see, is yours.'
I watch him down the slope.

A herb bruises underfoot letting its sharp scent
Tang the air like smoke.
A bird flutes sudden among the trees.
Higher I climb. Soft foliage flows away.
Below, houses and fields etch the plain.
I suck the air in sweet and warm with sun.

I will build here.
Prise up the sharp rocks, dig,
Sow flowers for bees.
The bird sings urgent in the highest branch.
Somewhere beyond treescreen
Water breaks into the light.
I slake my parched mouth at the full gush.

VII

After Ausonious

So I came late in the afternoon,
Sun going down as suns do
On the Northern frontier slow and burning,
My eyes gravelled with a day's riding
And a boy took my horse
In the rough clothes of those parts
While I stumbled into the house;
Oh call it house; four walls held off the night.
'You are a long way', the old man said,
'And the sun going down.
I do not think you have been this way before.'
He was I could see a fanatic
From some dank Western island the mist in his eyes,
Would have the heart out of your body
For his god. They have strange gods
Up here on the frontier of suffering and passion
Not to be bought with a formality
But demanding just the heart out of your body.
So I begged a room civilly
And there was none. Nothing though too good for me.
I must drink first and tear at some bread and meat
And make a little conversation among the rush lights
That the empire was falling, civilization tumbling
Like a summer clown in the market place
And we all bystanders. 'In the morning,' he said,
'I will show you my pride,'
And let me sleep at last heaped on a clay bed
While he tossed a little and settled to an old man's thin slumber.
With the grey light they woke us
Coming wolves through the pass.
The boy died when they burnt the stable
And the old man later of a grey grief.
'But first,' he said, 'my pride,'
And he had us carry him into the walled garden.
'They are nearly over but just one lingers
Under a finger of late sun.'
It was evening now, our second day there
And the men nervous, impatient to be gone,

43

But I humoured him.
Against the wall burning almost sullenly
As if it had sucked greedy on the day's sun
And now vibrated it into the sinking afternoon
A Paestum rose lady which you may treat as you will:
Make it a pot-pourri to sweeten our winter
Lifting summer and the garden into the early dusk,
Press it between the leaves of poems
Or wear it when you dance.
I have ridden hard to bring it with the last touch of light
Rouging the petalled skin like blood.

VIII

The Return

Time to be done with the props
That held the tunnel from tumbling about me.
Lingering I pack up
Letters, books, poems
Redolent of love
That lit me through my galleried night,
Chipping at the face of time
With insect persistence;
A deathwatch beetle knocking its way into light.

Like men too long underground
I have perhaps grown blind and dumb,
Cosset my comforters,
Shy back from the lifting cage
That jerks me out of the tomb.
Lazarus they say stumbled
Pounded by the sun.
The filmed eyes, dust cloaked tongue
Moved to pity.

Lay mouth on mouth:
That shall be miracle enough.

IX

He dreamed of Eldorado as a child:
The gilded boy, the sacrifice, priest-king,
The sacred valley no man ever found.
Grown he came at last
Overreaching the tides, between mountains,
Scrambling higher where eagles eyried
And flapped away in fear
That he should clutch and clamber for their perch.
Beyond the final pass the pinnacle
Where figures moved and trembled in the mist.
Sharp eyed with longing he trains his gaze
To stare into the high riding sun;
Sees a woman moving in a curtained room,
Hears voices, music;
Glasses shine, a bed is laid.
He shudders through the vision to beyond.

Alone on the rock slope
Knowing himself the golden boy
He dreams of La Dorada.
The pass he cannot cross
Is channelled through his heart.

X

The Letter

Times I am a child shut out
From the converse of adults.
The engraved phrases chiselled through long years,
Weathered now, bar me while I am solaced
With sweets and the talk goes on above my head.
Not that I question, only recognize
The enduring stones reared,
A portal I may not pass.

I peer tiptoe across the lettered sill,
Call you with prattle of rhymes,
Need, a tug at the skirts
But you are walking a high cella
Dedicated with ritual and poliphon
That you repeat word perfect.
I hold you and do not have you while the words intone.
Only your body cupped in my arms
Feeds me with our communion.

XI

Eurydice

'Take her then but never look back,'
The dire king-queen smiled, the ghosts drew close
Murmuring your name, their darling, on bloodless lips.
I am come playing among shades,
Dying for the death,
Move spectre through my days without you.

Give me your hand.
We climb upward through layered light.
Talk to me now so I can know you are here.
I am afraid of the dead with their paper mouths.
If I flinch your scenery trembles,
You sink away to shades
And I am left alone in the blaring sun.

Oh my dear, on another coast
Without you, engrieved,
The wild ones will tear my flesh,
My notes be drowned in the howl of the heart
Until I claim the dark kingdom as mine.
I will not look back.
I hear the whisper of following feet,
Feel the brush of your breath on my neck.
You come with me into the light.

XII

Unfathered the child clings to the wall of the heart:
The seed I cannot embed in your flesh sprouts in the mind
To tendril, leaf and flower while the unborn riot
Joyful in the parks and gardens of never will be.
I would watch you through nine months
Sail of our love together my ship and sea,
Where I swim free or am wave breaking on your shore,
Run up through the soft molluscular caverns of your body
And leave my ocean life limpet to the embrace
Of your flesh, so proud you can conceive my queen
Cat-walking stiff legged
Against our bellying burgeon of light.

There are things that can't be said,
Doors shut that I daren't push
Yet you open them freely with an 'if'
And 'I would like'.
Unused to presents, to precious awards,
I do not answer, stumble over jutting words.
Our children whisper in my head
But most that mothering you I glimpse by proxy
That I would penetrate, stir with my shuddering blood,
Walks in my dreams. I tender my eunuch rage,
The wooden sword that snaps on steel reason,
Yet know I am in you and the unborn children
Riot in our sun.

XIII

Post Coitum Triste Omne Animal

After love pain,
You turn away from me down a street
Suddenly picked bone clean to desolation,
Your face pale
After love.
I drive faster to wave
But already you are swallowed by the black gut
Of a taxi
And there is no pain love
Like parting after love.

All evening I shall go about
With the memory of your face below me
Greedy for words savoured,
Turned on the mind's questing tongue,
Wrung for comfort
Against the alien dream I inhabit.
All evening among dearfriend strangers
Watch you walk towards me
Across the naked floor,
Sink my bones in your phantom flesh
While the voices die to whispers.

After love pain my love
Yet after pain love.

XIV

All night on the cold plain under wrack of cloud
He has raged, driven wild by the ribboned flesh,
The claws that tore at the soft viscera,
Turning the crazed head to sink long teeth
Into his own hide and bloody the wounds afresh.
Kites hover blocking out the stars;
The lope of carrion dog shadows the hooves
That strike no sparks now from the flint fields.
Starting at his own flung black shape
He wantons on towards the abyss,
Shudders and sweats above the plunge
Where the rising sun will seethe the broken body,
Hatch corruption in the split blood
And the flies suck knowledge from the gaping sockets.

Afright that the hunters would some day come,
Rope and lead you away I sank in the green catstare,
Offered my heart to the punishing talons
And slashed you with my pain.
Gentle me now. This is the same field
Where we have wandered together,
Nuzzled among the lush clovers
And when you shiver, shying from the paddocks of light,
Gash me with the sharp edge of your fear,
I will cosset you among blossoms
Until we can stand without trembling.

XV

Gossiping by the fountain of Hel
The ladies contest the loves who pleasured them:
Genetrix, a kindle of children underfoot,
Sighs for the hard straight father of thousands;
Full-bubbed and buttocked Willandorf
Lays hand to thrusting hip
For the sharp piercing of the arrow man
Whose limbs are spars. Pandemos draws
The jostle of the bars, the one night stands,
The faceless lusts in unknown rooms;
Urania, pale with self-consuming flame
Unfed by flesh, dreams and does not speak.
They fill their pitchers with the gleaming words,
Splash heated cheeks with glistening images.
Paphia, Idalia, Cytherea, virgins and matrons:
Great ladies all, the faces of love.
But when she comes, Anadyomene
Putting off her searobe, they crowd close,
Listen while she whispers in the shell's ear
What seaboy tumbled overboard
Dolphin mounting, castaway on tideback,
Chased her laughing through the caverns of her blood
Or backed her up against the harbour wall
While dried leaves whickered in the thin night wind,
And warmed her with his mouth.

XVI

The city contains and is you.
Delving I learn a new archeology,
Uncover with gentle brushwork
The roots of sculpted façades
Colonnaded, ordered arias in stone.
Forgive me if somedays blunt, bulldozing
I rip at the tender earth,
Tear the landskip thoughts cinctured
Like a green belt drawn taut
Excluding those suburbs where you do not walk.
I would have you stand always
As if soil had no claim on you
While the elegant dancers move out and in
Threading the measured rooms
And I lay like warm sun on the honeyed walls.

'There is no more,' you say.
'I am not very good at being for long.'
And I surprise a swordblade sharp as today
That will bring the bright blood to my fingertips
Unless I sheathe it in my heart.
Gently I work with my trowel
Eroding the buried relics;
A broken toy, a handful of defaced coins,
The flawed glass; my treasures I dust
With my breath and cache with pride
Behind my eyes. Look below those mirrors
That give you back yourself.
You shall see them kept safe
And you may stand untroubled by the layered past
While the elegant dancers move out and in.

XVII

Prospect of Absence

Rocket on the dark sprays
Green foam flecks: aspirations
That must not be held in the hand
But let soar though they kindle the sheltering thatch.

We are burning my fear
That the light once down will not return,
That absence is forever
And you will come back with the stranger face
That is my death.

The head lolls and the painted eyes
Swivel as the sack crumples to ash.
Shovel him into the sparkbed.
Let him fly against the dark of departure.
Once, returning, I saw Orion jewelled and flaring
Through the winged porthole.

All stars shall plot you home.

XVIII

Nec penetrare et abire in corpus corpore toto

Now we have come to the white country
Where I have not been before
The light dizzies, the mind draws back.
'Lucretius was here,' you say.
I scan the coloured lines:
Feel the quick breath, moist mouth on mouth,
The hands that would tear the soft flesh.
He never came this far,
Stopped at the border there below
Where the commonwealth of loving ends.
You see his footprints as the snows begin
Falter and turn back.
Too rare this air for the curled nostril;
The sardonic lip pinches in the cold.
There you must leave your packs,
The comfort that love is all the same,
Step naked out of the body's warmth.

We lie unmoving, your hand stills on my back,
Only your eyes flicker.
Fearful I fret the silence with speech.
I have not been here before.
Other loves drove me, lusts rioted velvet and strident
But never this sounding hush,
The senses withdrawn, your flesh so much my own
I dream into your eyes without desire.
'Such love is always frustrate,' you say;
And I am alone on the white plateau.
Yet for a moment we stood blinded
In the pouring light while time fell back.

Though we run wanton through all colours of our spectrum
I will remember. And I have never been here before.

54

XIX

That the night never come,
The moon fall down
And the stars chill and go out;
Energy pall to aboriginal dust,
A lunarscape march with its glacier tread
Through valley and pass
Setting the bloodstream fast,
I, who cannot hold you by hostages of custom and flesh,
Weave chains, innocent as daisies
To bind, that will fade without the sun
Showering in the garden we have made our own,
Shrivel and powder under your feet
Like the ground bones of bird and mouse.

Winter stands outside.
Come in love. While the frost scythes
You bloom a white peony I gather in my arms,
Harvest in the dusky room,
Plunge my face in the heavy petals of belly and thigh,
Seek deep in the calyx mouth
Nectar in time of famine cold;
And we shall make blinding, beautiful gestures of love
Unfading as artifacts, as the rose that gilds our table.

XX

Perhaps it is better that I should not be able
To carry you up to the stars
Where we would constellate and confound
Their daily astronomy.

Perhaps it is better that other lands
Should not receive us burning
To weld their seasons into one long summer
And starve them with kissing.

Perhaps it is better that we should live by tasting,
Appetizers only that will not cloy
That this oh so rich feasting of pressed grape
And sweetmeat should never content.

Then why can I never accept it,
Fret earthbound, shiver in winter,
And rumble with fasting through the intoned masses
For you who are bread, cup, star and fire?

XXI

Learning how to cry
You breathe abdominally,
A sharp breath with open mouth;
A quivering, a faint quivering
Deep down in the abdomen.
The eyes moisten.
No image is needed; all purely physical.
Did you know that your eyes are moist all the time?
But that's the danger point.
As soon as you know it's coming
The eyes glaze, you lose it.
Like love, like coming.
Except that
Coming with you, in you,
Mind and body conjoin
In one wild crying.
I do not need to be taught.

XXII

And fondly expecting to find you everywhere
The pictures are full of you;
A graph of private reference:
Modigliani fleshed, Beardsley's fat woman,
A satirical duet we up and down the scale of love;
Fuseli's gothick fantasies to laugh your fear away,
Mares and foals nuzzling the unhuman light,
Parents resurrecting in our heads,
A girl Apollo on his back above the bed;
And every tone and tint of you.
The smiles of painted women
Are you galleried, an exposition I walk in
With loving laughter; a city conversation,
Duologue of fitted stones
To build arcady, tempio, or wren small churches
Octagon within square embellished,
Glorified, and you are hung
In every apse and alcove of my thought.

XXIII

Frond curled asleep she lies
Lapped between love and morning, light and light.
Sea strands of damp hair wrack the pillow
From the surf of kisses.
After the last tide
Our sweat dries salt in the shoals of her skin.
On a breathing shore she stirs in my arms
Puckering the closed anemone of her mouth
To mine and the lusting breakers
Bore through the sea lanes of my thighs
Spending themselves against the groins of love.

Watcher, I keep the hours at bay
That no scaled beast stalk her night,
Pirate her from my gift of dreams,
And in our morning beat on the smudged and drowsy lids
Relentless as furrowing waves.

XXIV

St Mary's, Harefield

Thanate, Thanate,
We have come in a wild afternoon,
The flung gold of October current in gutter and ditch,
Among these tombs shuttered to resurrection.
The Newdigates panoplied in red and black
Are urned and cherubinned against judgement,
Ours and theirs
And the huntsman on the outer wall who brought down
Small birds with his thunder
Appeases with the rightness of his rhyme.
Friesians chequer, a green swell
Is perfect in its parabola
And the chancel is gilded with children
Rehearsing another nativity.
We talk soundlessly of dead loves
Who are so much the living
In and through our love.
I tell a glum tale of an untended grave
And no marker.

Thanate, dark boy
Always you stand before
Reminding us of life but do not ask our worship.
You do not awe us with your imminence
Who die gladly crying into each other's mouths,
Who have no flowers for the dead
Only for the loving,
And at world's flashpoint,
Wing crumpling, skitter of tyres on a wet road,
Whatever holocaust should fire us
We would, our flesh charring breast to breast,
Outwit you Thanate; flame without fear.

Yet my blood cries not yet,
Only the sweet deaths we give each other
Without surfeit, the epitaphs
Woven through long hours of sighs and kisses.

I turn to look at you.
Shadows of raindrops from the car windows
Freckle your face like tears.
We will be spendthrift as autumn gold.
Leaves have no monuments
Except that we hold them in mind and tell of them.

This place is our pomp, our celebration,
Bought in the coining of our love.
Brother to sleep you shall not take it from us.

THE VENUS TOUCH

Snowtime

I make for you in snowtime a poem
Simple as the figures children build,
Father or lover, with upturned smiling mouth
And the gleam of faceted eyes,
To stand beyond your window after dark
Among the arrow prints of birds
And the hung fleece of leaves,
The moulded lines firm and strong,
For the child in you to clap hands,
Lead me wondering into the garden;
And I make it out of the white drift of love.

Oh Penelope, what did you do?
Slip a corn dolly between the sheets
In likeness of a man?
Straw coloured hair, o fair
Achaen, and the eyes you might have made
Of some island speedwell.
Did you talk to it as you loomed
A warp of a life, were you faithful
To its unanswering fixed stare
That might have been anyone's,
The clamourers in the courtyard,
Jove come down, a passing pedlar
With ballads of his own pain?

I wouldn't have blamed you.
Times among the flat fields
I lost your face. I knew I loved
And your name but it had
No lineaments and that was Persephone's
Hour who never wanted me till I had you
Then took all shapes to lead me from my course.
I am come home but the shutters are down
In that house, all asleep
While the beggar lingers outside
Nursing his scar, the wound of love
You branded into his flesh.

Let me walk in your dreams
And tomorrow again I will draw
My bow at your venture, run up
Your steps and drive our shadows
Mewling into the dark.

Tutto Tremante

Thinking on three who trembled:
Sappho alone at midnight pale as winter grass,
The roseboy struck to the bone with chill ever after,
Paolo betrayed by imagination, wordspell,
And her mouth, her mouth,
I question if their thighs ached as mine do,
Their breath clotted so thick in the throat,
Desire flushed like gall in the gut
Still after this time passed
When we cling crying to each other,
Die, resurrect to die again; still, still,
After a day's tombed eternity,
I am all trembling for you.

Should I wear masks for you?
Should I counterfeit and strut on the stage of myself,
Suspend your disbelief with play?

I am all lovers; in me their lines meet
Or in your infinity who are all queens
Divinely right. So we lift them
From the flat page, endow with shape and colour
And the dimension of love;
Make of their temporal our long present,
Rehearse, repeat the gestures, phrases
Compounded of lust and tenderness.
Only do not look at me like that
Or I forget my words.

Stand with me now at the death of the year
Where we first loved.
Though they lay pennies on its eyes,
Wind it with oblivion and earth it deep
The grave figures are hatched on our hearts
And start green from the soil
With every day's new Spring.

Say again we have built an empire,
That our white sphere outlives mere kingdoms;
For immortality. Lay all seige to us
Our walls are battlemented,
No little wicked gate lets out a traitor
Since we are citizens and emperors
That rule tenderly in each other's weal.

I am love's fool, clown for you,
Divert your days, antic and stumbling;
Tumble the bauble my heart
For your delight. If you smile
I am rewarded, paid in your pleasure,
The soft cries that bring me down
Hawk to your trembling.

You, love's garner, hold our harvest
In your arms. Our joy runs in your mild flesh
Warm as milk, nurturing us both.
Spent I rock in the bay of belly and breasts,
Am gathered and held while you kiss me to life
Til I am sword again, the devourer
Who would eat your heart.

Let this duality swing between us,
Our sacrament, giving and given.
Be my autumn, I your fierce summer;
My winter dying you wake to Spring.
So we shall turn and turn on love
As easy as blending months or the to and fro of tides
And never go lonely into new year again.

Stand with me then. They are tolling for us
A death and a birth who are ever
Dying and reborn, who are bound
Out of time and all passing.
Give me your hand. We will write on this stone
In letters heart deep that all may know
Marvelling how we love.

Tzarskoë Selo

Not that I love you more when snow falls;
That would be to make the heart seasonal,
Determined by time and place,
Yet you are my winter palace
Of agate and marble,
And I wonder in your rooms,

Cap in hand, that the guards should let me in,
Take my dull coins as currency,
Allow my muddy boots to track
The fretted floors;
Let me finger the damask bed-hangings,
Baldacchinoed high altar where we perform our rites
Stare unwashed into the bath-house,
Leave breadcrumbs among the silver
And blackprint the courtyard's purity;
Inherit riches my tongue stumbles over
Like a child at a party with too much cake
Who cannot say thankyou and, 'I like it.'

Always you surprise me, mouth agape,
In some far chamber where the public are forbidden
Happen upon me, winter queen jewelled and reigning
When I have nothing to offer but homage
And the snowball in my hand.

Legends

One   Cherubino

Knowing he loved her more than children should
They packed him off to fight;
The foreign wars would make a man of him.
That steel severance took him in the heart.
They brought him girls and mocked him
To be brave. Perhaps he wrote
From his billet in the town,
'Madam, I commend . . .' and wept,
And drank; the cherub lad become a soldier shell.
No history tells us
How the blank days failed for her.

Made man they sent him back. Masked
He enters the swaying hall,
Searches the dancers for remembered eyes,
A gesture. Leads her willingly away.
Remembering she cries on love.
Her voice, echoing in the sac that held his heart,
Provokes to lust. Beyond the long windows,
In the glittering garden, the marble death
Stirs to embrace them both.

Two Guenever

Six weeks he lingered, shrunk on salt tears
And fasting two span from that first height
That would have overtopped the world
For her. They laid him in her bier
To bury him. That final parting:
All day she walked knowing he would be there
Suddenly, lifting her eyes swooned and then,
Her last bitch trick he saw through,

Loved her for: 'Have bliss of someone else.
You never will keep faith.'
But dared not kiss him
And dying prayed two days never to see
His face again since that flame,
That envy fanned to war, leapt in her still.

So he went away bound her captive,
Glad in his chains as he had always been.
And the sweet fragrance his body held
That we hanker after, reading between the lines,
Know it the distillation of their love.

Between you and me
Lie the childhood images
Playing out mothers and fathers
Patterns of loving
On a wet afternoon.

Between you and I
Two egos stand
Defying the grammar of the heart
In tactical attitudes
Pretentiously incorrect.

Between us
There is nothing but love
An indivisible object
Where both are subject
Entwined without accusation.

Between there is nothing but love.

Allegory

Frail child you wept yourself to sleep,
The silk string snapped.
Carnivorous, cloven footed
The centaurs rage through arcady;
Lovers and poets cower among the rocks:
Strumpetted, assailed the goddess swoons,
Thrust back by the coarse hands, blackly overhung;
Her sweet flesh vulture prey,
Mere carrion. Adonis gored bleeds into the dust.

Accept this litany. By all the live dead
Who held in word or line
The flimsy barricade against that tyranny,
Opposed with their quick breath
The oligarch destruction and dying,
Shot down in the public square,
Among debris of torn tissue
Delicate as insect wing,
Proclaimed and yet we live;
Over whom we raise slight temples
Of our longing and faith
Intangible as moonlight,
By these presents I conjure you
Grow strong, winged again.

You have taught us your songs,
Pierced us til we bleed ambrosia.
Rarefied among your stars we cannot live
On the weighted earth where the days die
Anonymous, unmarked.

Listen, I wake you; mend up your bow.
We wipe your tears. Sleeping a little,
You dreamed we walked hand in hand
Through smiles among the painted sunlight
While nymphs crept out of the trees.
It shall be so.

Habits

You didn't turn at the door:
A habit broken that might have impaled us
On repetition, that not turning
I might think, 'What did she mean?'
Or the act become a formality
When none can muffle the sound
Of tearing flesh.
So we break habits deliberately
Like priceless vases dropped
On a concrete floor to show
We can stand the shock, have courage
To take the symbol and throw it away.

Yet there are habits less easily fractured.
The habit of being without you
Once broken doesn't mend so soon;
I plug the gap with drink and talk
Yet every echo uncovers the void
That is always there, that I hide,
Camouflage with light and shade of gossip
Lest stumbling you glimpse the depths
That house me apart and take fright.

Torn I tack it together; a botched job
Cobbled up with cat's teeth but it will do
Unless you should break the habit of loving me,
The seams tear open and I tumble headlong into dark.

You sleep now, my self in your arms.
My weight lies smooth, heavy
Between your breasts and thighs.
Homeless my thoughts wander the city,
Walk the waters of Thames,
Light as others' dreams.

Feel that quick touch?
That was my mouth on yours.

Ghost, unfleshed since you hold my substance
I am all air and fire;
All water too, liquefy in tears
Like classic heroes who wept unshamed
At love or fate.

'Why out so late?' They stop me
In the street, shine torches in my eyes.
Revenant, unhoused I stammer blind.
'No fixed abode?' Their notebooks poise.
Tell them I have a lodging close at hand;
Surety, bond; that doors stand wide for me
And, with daylight, you will take me in.

Last night, oh last night
I was Antony, emperor.
Tonight the climbing boy creeps snivelling
To his sack in the corner
And there is no coverlet flesh
To keep out the draughts.

'Nessun maggior dolore,'

They remembering that bliss they missed,
When the age was golden,
Rose daily along the pathways of smiles,
Was harnessed to thundering light,
Called that the greatest pain
Yet endured and love never left them.
Still they wandered hell together
Though pared to shades
As I would do always
That we might not be divided.

But now let us take back our sun.

It is as though, swopping remembrances
Many coloured as a bag of marbles,
Songs and comics, we had been
Children together yet I know
We would never have met.
Ranging the backchats I was some
Wild creature you weren't allowed to play with,
Hunted with the rough pack,
Hallooing like Tarzan into the dusk
And didn't wear socks.
Did you ever, I wonder, look out
Beyond your driveway where the swart shapes
Capered under the lamp? Does your compassion
For dumb beasts date from this time?

Even then I loved you. Knew before
You showed me the turretted house,
On an afternoon of windy visitation
When the streets were torn open with winter,
I drank tea, you coffee
Reminding us we would never have met,
That you were the Rapunzel I imaged
When the gang had gone home to bed
And I was left scuffing my boots

Alone, looking in through lit windows
Where the angel fish trailed their lace doyleys
In the bought sunlight of their tropical tank.
You were imprisoned, I knew,
Or else you would come out and play
And I should rescue you but you must
Let down your hair for me to climb up.
No one would say which window held you.

Later we might have met learning
But again I could have loved you
Only in the distance, written you poems,
Followed you home dawdling well back,
The immutable class laws of children,
'She's in the Upper Fifth, you're only in Lower Four,'
Keeping us apart still.

So I have pursued you impossibly
Under all guises, dragging behind
Til last you turned and let me catch up;
Let fall that ladder to mount,
Possess your castle. It's good
To be grown up. 'Now no one
Can stop us playing together.'
Our games are more innocent than children's.

Tell me a story.
Let there be dragons and ogres
For I am used to them;
A unicorn who gave himself up for a lady,
Horned in on captivity,
And shot his bolt.
But let it be alright
In the end.

Tell me a story
While we lie embedded in each other's arms,
My mouth in your hair
So I hold my breath with listening
And the words fall, sonorous caresses,
On my head. The Spring afternoon
Draws mild curtains across our windows
Of woven rain and sunwarp.

Tell me your story
And I will weep or laugh.
The syllables spell us a charm for healing,
Bind our sore places with webs
And moonshine, exorcise.
Bereaved children we follow
Each other's wanderings.
There was once a princess . . .

The woodcutter loved her.
Such tales are true.

Bernini's St Theresa

one

Her shuddering angel scattering light like sperm,
Air upborne with goldtipped arrow poised,
Whose smiles beat down her shuttered eyes,
Engenders ecstasy; subject she lies
Bound with her heart strings
While the molten tides flush through her thighs.
Lips part to let those cries
Break in prayers, not sighs.

How can her seraph,
Dazed with her rending softness,
Whose mouth has sucked the salt weep
Of her wound that dart provokes, like milk,
Play again among cherubs,
Children; announce to virgins
The triumph of harrowing flame?

two

Some darksoul nights her seraph does not come.
'Crucified between heaven and earth,'
Limbo held she waits
His resurrection.
Fallen, hell-bent, he droops.
Those pinions lank with tears
Cannot vault him
Over the walls of light.
Dull iron blunts his spear.
The bloodied shadows dance across his eyes
Mocking that bliss, that breast,
Her ecstasy he made his own.
Lured by their joy he hammers at her door
Plunging the crude shaft
Again, again into her flesh;
Her moans, not rapture but sharp pain,
Drive off their heaven
And hurl him Icarus down
Who dared the sun.

Become her torment dark angel
Beats back the soft arms
That would catch him close,
Hold him serene in that white drift
Where he might lay his mouth,
Suck peace sweet as milk;
His pain a lash fiercer
Than any whip until she falls trembling.
Her last breath, his kiss to life
She gives him out of love,
Stirs the bedraggled plumes,
Rising he puts on light,
Invests them in his rays.
Fire-tipped she takes him swooning to herself,
Brided, broken, giving, given,
And who shall tell their ecstasy apart?

Der Rosenkavalier

one

The footmen are in league
So do not trust them.
Malice or sloth cancel out your wage.
A barbershop quartet they watched him through the window,
Ready with soft soap or the knife,
And tittered while he pressed
His forehead to the horse's flank,
Seeing the road scurry under the hooves,
The years of Sunday roasts,
The lusts in three-four time;
Prayed she would call him back
Then rode away unarmed.

Your fears report you lonely.
Do not believe them.
In our play all roles are doubled:
It is also you I bring the silver rose.

two

Tonight he sleeps away. She rises
To stop the clocks and hold up time;
No pause for the gilt and wanton loves
That smile their chiding. The hand
Trembles over the inexorable faces.
Tomorrow at her toilet she will pluck
A silver hair and shrink from the wizened
Sadness of the pet ape. Her lover hunts her
Through the corridors of years. Poor ghost,
She flits from room to room in the small hours,
Insubstantial as chiffon
Crying, 'You can never catch me.'

Stand still. Turn to face him.
He too grows old in your footsteps,
Dragging your despair. Submit to love.
In all dying our ages are the same.

three

Imp you first attend the lady,
Bring her breakfast, restoratives
After a night of love,
Make straight, lay out her mask
While he skulks behind the bedcurtains,
Trailing his sword.
Bearer of love, go-between,
She sends you with his last commission,
Dismissed. Only in the last act
She would have you follow her still
But you are alone on stage
And dance away with a wisp of handkerchief.

Let her look for a new servant;
She will not find one so brisk, so meet
To her command. That other child,
Paleface, languorous will unsurp your place.

four

He was proud being young,
Took his hurt out into the street
And rode away. He was wrong
Being young. Did he think
She might send after him, call him
Back, or feel God and custom
A windmill he could not tilt?
His wound bled slow. Dried blood
Feeds roses. Three times he calls her,
'Marie Thérèse,' an invocation that
Cannot bring her close. He stands between,
Equidistant in the trio while she soars.
I learn from him. No pride shall spur me
Out of sight. I will not leave that room:
The casket cannot hold my petalled heart.
I am too old to play she loves me not.

Eurydice II

Dead hands jealous some days drew her back.
Gathering flowers she stopped;
Earth opened, that chariot stood ready,
Funeral horses tossed their hearse black plumes,
Mutely the dark king beckoned
Her sullen feet.

In the empty house he hears
The hush in the garden,
The song her heart sang towards him stilled,
Runs from the room hurling his frantic notes
Into the air to stay that flight.
Fiercely he holds her; the earth closes.

Yet if it were all to do again:
Charon, Cerberus, the manyheaded dead,
He would take his terror and his pocketful
Of rhymes, fling down the scraps of love
To fill that maw; bribe, busk or plead
And drive her stumbling up towards the sun.

Limbo

In Limboland they wait
Who are neither living nor dead
But beyond grace;
For whom eternity passes without presence.
So I inhabit for a time this negative,
Knowing that you too are walking apart
Among your dead,
Until my saint summon me
With your speaking eyes
And I put on redemption
With your flesh.

Epistle

Once
There was a time,
The calendar tells me,
When we were not,
When this so present was future
And the past a range
Of crooked queries marking off the years.
Call it the dreamtime
For there was nothing about it of Eden;
Was aboriginal, mist-shaped,
Myself someone who never dreamed in colour.
Since my birth I hardly remember it
Except when its fears overtake me
Alone, afraid of the dark, and I scurry
To placate those malign spirits
With gravings of your name
On rocks and pictures of lovers
Done in my own blood.
Sometimes then I thought I glimpsed you
But it was only the mirage of my own desire
Dancing away over the naked plain
And withdrew to vanishing point
When I tried to come close.
Today, our birthday, I would not
Burden with hung symbols
When all are feastdays, holydays
But to say look at me love
With those eyes that starred our nativity
Only clearer by a year.
They show me all the colours of loving
And all my life is present on your breast.

When I was young I used to sleep
On the bare ground, spreadeagled
In the sun, my face against the coarse grass hair,
Imagining the ooze of tiredness
Seep down from my pores through fibres, topsoil,
Slither over the unwilling clay to be sopped up
At last by the indifferent compassion of chalk.

Now, my cheek bedded soft in your hair,
I straddle your warm earth,
Know the ache in the heart's bones
Eased by your arms; the rise
And fall of your breath surf soothe
All abrasions and the scrutiny of your love
Hold me safefast while I sleep.

Let fall from love you take
Such postures as Titian,
Correggio, Giorgione
Stroked for Danäe, Antiope,
Venus; seeded by gold shower,
Satyrized sleeping, fucked drowsy
An arm under her head
As white roses heavy with bees'
Predations droop blowsed petals,
Lambent under the full lips of the sun;
Display their pistil wounds
Where bruising tongues
Filched honey while they smiled.
Generous of yourself you offer
Curving perspectives, limbs sagged under love,
To progress with eyes, hands, mouth
While you lie open, falling as
Water, sunlight, petals.

That running upstairs child you deprecate,
Would banish back down your years,
Cries to me sometimes, 'Lost!'
From the vertigo of dreams.
'That door, was it left or right?
Where was time while I bent my head
Over the album, the coloured names
Carrying me away?' I stretch a hand,
Knowing the least hair's fall,
To that child loved always for the woman
Who last night cried wild in my arms,
Swept beyond yourself and running
Up stair and stair to joy.

Picture's end. Across the split mouth of the screen
Hero and heroine, stumbling a little
Under the burden of our hope, run,
Arms spread to catch up our hearts
And hold them between rehearsed lips.
In the moist wombdark where others sit alone
With their dreams I clench your hand
Whose warmsilk contours I have kneaded,
Traced the cuticle ridges, stabbed myself
To pain pleasure on the cat point nails,
Stuck fast in our sweated balm,
Through their reeling saga of lost and found.
The lights spot out the unshamed glitter
Oh my cheeks. All hours away
I run towards you with my burden hope,
Arms stretched on emptiness,
Air slipstreaming through my hollow bones,
To consummation on your mouth
And our saga's beginning.

There is no balm. The time apart
Bleeds slow and thick still
And will not be sutured
With tendrils of music,
Bound with soft words remembered.
You walk away in my head,
Scuff up my quick loss
As children's uncaring shoes
The leaves of our second autumn,
Crossing the road head up
So you may not see the damply clinging shapes
That would clog your feet.

The labyrinth hours tunnel ahead
Through which I follow the unwinding of
The lover's knot my saint
Placed in my hands to guide me
While the minotaur bellows in my dark.
Yet he shall not have me.
Legend is on my side.
Bedded in our enchanted island,
Myself, the fierce god, shall comfort you,
Roaring through your dark,
For all desertions.

The poor sod in the next cell
Is breaking up his bed.
I hear his tears and rage,
The impotent grief
Of a wild thing new trapped.
'Can't do his bird,'
The screw grins through portcullis teeth.

Before he was limed
His bird down in his arms
Beat against his caging ribs,
Fluttering her cries soft into his mouth
As he stroked her dying,
A canary set in the sun.

'Can't do his bird.'
Should be patient,
Take it like a man.
I hammer warder on his door,
'Shut up in there.'

'Oh my dove, my heart,'
I hear him weep and
The voice is my own,
Not even the thickness of skin between us,
These my hands abraded on the unanswering stone.

Though you hide under mountains
The same pain torments us.
I know when you wince
By the contraction of my heart.

Shisaku in snow:
I press up into your ice
Lake and you fall on
Me in white flakes. Hot love words.

You shall not ever, my love,
Be left to wander lost
Down that white dream road.
I am the scarecrow at
Your furthest vision
Who holds out arms to bar
And hold you. I am
The feet running behind
That will not let you stray.
Daedelus on my strong wings
I bear us home while you are couched
Warm among my plumes,
Your cheek laid to my neck.
Soon I shall lead you again
To the eternity of our bed.
I will never let you go.

Sleep

Twin brother to death you have
His looks, hooded, featureless,
'Before me,' you say, 'all men are passive,
Fall back under my weight
Heavy lidding their eyes, sink.
Why should you strive against me?'

Beast you take her from me,
Ravish her into dreams
Where I cannot Perseus hover
Putting out dragons nor even an arm
To hold her when she weeps
Naked to demons under your spell.

You part us daily. Leave me
Adrift in Acheron doubting if daylight
Will ferry me back to life.
Curtains shrouding the window
Are blazoned with dogs' heads
That would keep me from crossing that river

Oh sweet sour Thames where my love
Might glide in apotheosis of sunrise,
Blood and gold. I take against you
These words. After three days sleepless
Men die. I toss and turn
And will not let you in.

Or if I do start waking
In that prime hour of lovers, mystics,
Small animals who seek their heart,
Their hunger in your despite,
Weeping alone in their narrow beds,
Burrows, small salt pearls
That may, like this, be any price.

Triptych

And out of this unspilt seed,
Those that cannot be mine
Bourne in your billowing sail
My piracy stormed,
I offer you pearls, tears
You will not shed
For that daughter I love
In your belly or the cradle of your arms,
Knowing you must let her go
To other lovers like me.

I with neither past nor future
But only your present
Frescoed day by day,
Blocking in our design,
Stretch to you, aureoled for me
In that descending order
Midway in the triptych
Mothers and daughters,
Purgatoria, my saint, madonna,
Hands that would soothe
Your past and future into our present
Canopying you with my love
Through the long night apart.

Graphics for St. Valentine

ice crystals etch your
name on this glass to erase
it splinter my heart.

love all devourer
wolfs music image word yet
hungers for your flesh.

sucking to the rind
each minute of you honeyed
fruit I waste for more.

heavy eyed we sit
unwilling that night should rear
itself between us.

Logically from John Donne

Driving away from you is
Always to be night
Driving East into setting
Sun under branches
Black between waters through park
Where last night you said,
'O beautiful it is this
City and our love.'
No, not twilight. Full dark falls
Numbing as thunder
Clap at once tropical and
Arctic so that this
Paradox of driving East
Into day's fall is
Heart's syllogism; this end
Inherent in that
Premise: we love, and to be
Absent is to be
Gone West, benighted; homing
Is into sunrise
By ratiocination
Of blood since you are
Lodestar, compass. I would drive
Our sun's chrome bright car
In reverse with wild horse power,
My desires, til I brake
Stand shuddering at your door.

Magritte Catalogue

I recognise this landscape,
Have inhabited these dead surfaces
For no one lives here,
All are travellers passing through
Or guests merely in some bleak
Boarding house where time is transfixed,
Doors and casements keyhole on blackness,
A comb, alien and titan, usurps the bed.
Home is always elsewhere
Guilt haunted; the ideal,
Cotton wool clouds on baby blue,
Is the eye's false image;
Reality and art confound in the canvas pane
Both irrelevant. Only wit
Sees us through: a golden manna
Of French bread.

I have leant on the parapet
Of a dawn bridge, blackwinged,
Or walked my corpse at night
By beckoning water; gone towards pleasure
While myself turned away.
Today revoking that past
In the detritus of living, bills, letters
Beaucoup de souvenirs, I scented
Terror: that drowned cadaver
Would clasp and drag me under.
But it was another, an old country.
In this land where you walk with me
Light echoes from planes textured
Soft as your mouth, vibrates in
The laughter of kisses, is
Oh alive.

Lines to go with a Lily

Yellow trumpets
Annunciate the year's resurrection
From every corner barrow
And I poise
Letting love fall about me
Like sunlight
On the threshold of our third summer
Telling you drop the chaste ice chains
Winter links about your heart,
Open to the knock
Of this stave
Tender yet obstinate
As daffodils
And bear our joy, my pride,
Before you
Swelling with our Spring.

Wishing to erect for you
In grave lines some headstone
Cusped with cupidons,
And heads-I-win with
Bifronting Janus
As children build castles
Crying, 'Come see before the waves
Lay down our mortality,
Our aspiration on the pebbled shore,'
Some prompter to rehearse
Our two-year sovereignty
For your applause,

I stub bare feet on the knowledge
That for you time runs
Neither backwards nor forwards;
Is instant now. I watch you
Building in this sunlight,
Sculpting from golden fragments,
And lug my marker far out
Across the puddled sand
To where the tide lies back.
See, those amoretti are heaping
Our seawall, laughing in the ripples.
You can play here safe til nightfall.

Aria for Midsummer's Eve

Extol me her midsummer flesh,
Lay your praises over the wounds of absence,
Poultice of dew heavy leaves from the dream wood;
Wordspell solace.

All charms are hers. On this eve
Arias sing about her; there is wine
And strawberries by the water where queen
She leans and smiles.

Alone I wrench time and layer
Days and nights, sweet and sour, in my angel cake
Of loving since our clock has no hands,
Ours is ever,

And our occasions hang gauzing
Each other; this year last though absent I
Page beside you over the lawns, pin up
Froth of hedge lace

The white folds at your breast I traced,
Limning its silk swags' moondrawn swell as if
You lay pregnant with our high summer love,
Last night abed,

Span your belly with a warming hand
Yet double vision you driving home under
A night sieved with stars or late plucking for me
Dogrose kisses.

I am beset with a dream of fair woman,
Lunatic for Venus flesh
So sweet in the night
I do not know if I have woven her,
Pygmalion, out of my desires
Or if indeed those hours she lay
Beside, under me.
Happy the hand that touches her,
The cloth that drapes her,
The eyes and words that catch hers.
Where she is the skies are
Clouded with loves, the minutes dove drawn.
I whimper in this waking sleep
Remembering as dogs run down past quarry,
Hunter and snared by my dreams of fair woman,
Lunatic for your Venus Flesh.

Haikus

Starved a week for your
Body I glut on glimpsed sweets
Your breast between folds.

If you would leave me
Be as we are with old dogs
Kind, sweet kill me first.

Daphnis and Chloe
Apart at night wept. Their dawn
Rose faster than mine.

Bastard siblings I
Father on absence that trull
I suffer when she, joy,
Is away, my poems,
When we look babies,
My eyes plunged in hers,
We make strong children
Of laughter that run off
Nimble as our time
Together with no
Need of nursery rhymes
To rock their puling.

Bed whose sheets she chose
Tiepoloed with sunrise,
My aurora, where two nights
I lay in cloudy bliss, hero's hand
Shielding her breast, limbs lapping
Hers as the rough calyx
The wantonness of silk corolla,
Tonight I stretch my arms
Through your wastes become
Unyielding as pink marble,
Verona's paving stones in chill dawn,
Capulet's tomb, and hanker
For that other hard narrow cot
Where we lovered
Short hours till she slept,
Her breath coming and going
On my cheek as Eros fanned
Venus and Mars, murmuring me,
Her face child smoothed by my lips,
Cupid's kisses, scented as violet
Cachous as I watchdogged her dreams.
Bed, tonight you are too wide;
Your pillowy flesh no comfort.
My bones ache and toss in your chaste unease.

A Litany for St Venus del Parto, Monterchi

My lady of the bursting belly
Split like a ripe fruit,
Chestnut, tomato,
In this poured gold morning
As if all autumn were your
Gathered festival,
The palanquin held open before you,
Figured with maidenhair tendrils,
Is the lips of your own sweet part
O where I Gabriel
Fucked you with a lily
That you may scatter light seeds,
My fecund goddess,
Venus genetrix,
In men's minds.

No wonder if the dead lie at your feet;
Do we not blazon
Tombs with cupids in
Token of resurrection,
Knowing that only love can
Put out death? Black
Cypresses brushing their cameos on
The horizon are everlasting,
Shed no gilt poplar patina.
Let the dead bury the dead.
Calmly your hand unpicks a seam
Like Caesar's or a ripped pea
Pod that you may dream
Virgin unbroken,
Ma donna.

You cannot fool me with your simple
Blue dress cut elegant
As a queen's (an old trick
Madam, and this veil over
My eyes so that the day aches
With you and brilliance)
Nor the peasant women wanting lovers

Who have brought you oblations
To this fane longer than your picture
Has reigned serene in its white shrine;
You are only a girl, a child
Even sometimes in my arms,
Yet I know you too,
Goddess, whore, mother,
And adore you.

Chinoiseries

1.Autumn

Sparrows and leaves fall in the garden,
Burnt paper of birds, bronze foil
Of foliage, dying year's tokens.

If I were stout, rich with empire's spoils
I would build you a pavilion
Whose walls, like in the story, rang with bells.

And we should make love under a dragon
In a four-poster with brass gong rails;
Your toes would be poppy-sleep vermilion;

Your fingers lacquered sagest green. Nightingales
Of gold and lapis lazuli whose song
Might soothe dying emperors would tell

Our lyric love new through all seasons.
But instead I build paper halls
While music drops its scales, reeling

Cathay and Tartary in fluted scrolls
On the air: a princess and prince unknown
Impersonate us, save us their toils

While outside leaves transpare to gold, beaten
By sun and another year's first cold.
I take all this to tell you it is autumn

2. Fable

And when the princess was sick
The beggerman who was of course
A prince in disguise (or was it
The other way round?) came
And lay down across her threshold
Where she slept in silk
So that his heart might keep beating
For both of them if hers should stop
And their breath come and go together.
'You are an extremist,' they said.
To which he answered,
'Our lives are too short for anything less.'

Then you awoke with the fever gone
And I lifted my snout from between
Teardamp paws (your dog, highness),
Rushing at you with nuzzle of kisses
And this paper of old news
That headlines my love.

3. Willow Pattern Plate

I was brought up on Woolworth's willow pattern.
Slices of bread and sugar hid
The blue and white characters.
As you consumed their sweet pap
(Remember grit of granulated crystals
Between the teeth?)
You laid love bare.
I knew it was love
Because of the bluebirds
Skylarking with a ribbon
Up above the bridge
And the lovers were easy to decipher
Under the crumbs and candied flaws.
But the three old men were don'ts,
Strictures: Not-too-much, Not-too-often,
Not-for-ever; the last slice revealed
A whole round puzzle
That no one could explain.
Early you see I was hooked
On love and sweetness,
Ruining my teeth and me together
On a threepenny and sixpenny promise,
Conditioned to expect the two in one,
Though I never found them before,
Only now as we hurry towards each other
I understand that Chinese puzzle:
The old men are ugly and liars
Who can't stop us meeting
On that bridge over the river's laughter
And your love is sweetness on my tongue.

4. Small Pieces of Jade

The much lusted after
Face of our national courtesan
Does not stir me, nor her body.
Can it be that I am growing old?
Or have you so spoiled my palate
For other women?
One thing is certain:
Without you I should starve to death.
                    *
What should I do but stare
At your bedroom window
While the white moon
Stares at me? The light goes out.
Passersby look up curiously
For a moment then away
As I try to disguise my presence
With an appearance of purpose.
It may be I am as pale
As that moon.
                    *
You have been gone four years.
So it is though a lying clock
Would say four hours. Tell me
You who tick off my heartbeats
As seconds, who cause seasons
To change in your face,
Who hold me unflickering light years
With those lodestars your eyes
Or draw my tides
With your bellying moon
How is it, mistress of my time,
Our together runs, runs?
                    *
If I were the little gold fish
We bought today, articulated,
I would swim up the soft canal
Of your body and plash and play
In the deep of you.
Instead, articulate, I send
Shoals of minnow rhymes
To spawn in your head.

5. Drinking Song

Wine is only good when you are not
In love. I have poured in my time
Libations enough, troubling the cots
Of the dead with my hiccups on life.

Across the street they are plucking strings
While I settle the arm of the squat black
Telephone toad on its haunches. It sings
No more with her notes. Throw it back

To sink in a witch's ooze till she
Call me again. Useless the crimson
Cup, perfume of the cassia tree,
Silk screens and hands to beckon me in.

Wine is only good without love,
Without yearning that will vinegar it fast.
Let me lie drunk there, my mouth not move
From the goblet of her white jade breast.

6. Old Age

I find nothing but regret in the sages:
Rahaku in exile,
Po Chü-i recalling a lost daughter;
Threnodies on youth and exhortations
To patience without conviction;
Laments for the unstrung bow,
The failed strength of bowmen;
Girls bathing, green flesh
Under a shower of scooped pearls
Over naked shoulder and breast
While the boys, young warriors,
Curvet out of the bushes.
Age brought them only the delicious
Pain of remembering: 'Time has taken . . .
And comes no more Spring,
The snows melting, the girl and glass
We shared.'

Sages you have nothing to tell me;
My regrets aren't yours;
Only that I have not loved her
Half a lifetime, that Spring
Passed in a hide and seek where I hunted
Always in the dark. Perhaps it served
The heart's apprenticeship; I was
Being made worthy, mastering
This fine art, firm and delicate
As brushwork, to pleasure her.
Read me no more dry tales of pale youth,
Thwarted ambition, lost places.
Now in my second childhood
She is all countries I would wish to see,
All aspirations and our desire
Passion fruit eaten out of the tin
With a spoon.

Nocturnal for the Winter Solstice

Yesterday, Lucy's forever now,
Shortest though old style your calendar
   Gave a different figure
   Primed with ill luck black enough,
     You might well have thought,
For perpetual mourning, I forgot,
I confess, your obsequies. Unsought
By my usual pilgrim and limping feet,
Grave divine, I offer you this chaplet.

Many times if it had not been for you,
Sir, there in your shroud I couldn't have gone on.
   Your death and hers (whichever one
   Of your gleaming mistresses so
     The object of my worship,
By your proxy favour gone in to trip
A three hundred-year-old measure I slipped
My, your hand to in valediction)
Gave me possibility to live on.

Always at this dropsical season,
Swollen for a nativity not mine
   Like the laid bare belly of an
   Old queen, glutted on faith not reason,
     That lank dogend of a day
Stood me at your elbow, my wreath awry,
Rigid as your marble bones in fancy;
Become stoic in a despair that then
Could not, unliving, die with you again.

I have been your chantry, rehearsed psalms
For your undying lines. Now I must go.
   Give me my indenture. Below
   My neighbours spit on their palms
     For luck and strife but I
Am made in her perpetuity
Master of love who have sought, taught by thee,
Baroque puritan, an aesthetic
Manifest at last in her white fleshed spirit.

Watch with me this little death, this night,
Our wake. Tomorrow my sun renews.
  I have been long, love knows,
  Affected by dreams of saints:
    Magdalen, Thérèse,
Mary, pursued mirages that cease
In her who is all my desert's oasis.
You will forgive me begun so late
That now I only keep time for her days.

Last eve, I boast, I made vigil on her shrine,
Prostrate in our devotions without thought
  Of any death except ours bought
  With our antiphony of crying;
    A death for a death.
You will not be unsung but my breath
Grows shorter and is spent in kisses not grief.
Deep in the solstice of our love we forgot,
I hear you applaud, yours and the world's midnight.

A Baked Potato

Something to take away. Nightshift then:
Going off with my bag of snap to drop
Down the long shaft of evening to the black seams
Of sleep where all night I hack out dreams,
Jet gems, fossils, dead things and, lucky sometimes,
A vein of fool's gold, a glint of you,
With one eye always on the little bird,
Your heart, I carry in my ribcage,
Lest it fall dead and me too.

Oh let no one creep into my bed, your flesh,
While I toil away (no sweated sweet labour
Such as I mine in you); that bird
Trill to me with your remembered tongue.
My own fears poison the air. I hold
Your put-up love warm in my hands
For luck and comfort as the cage goes down.

Mal or I

If I loved you less than
Tristram Iseult
This edge of separation
Might lie blunt
Between us.

Yesterday we hurt ourselves
Unable to make love we opened
The pains in our wrists
And let out the mounting blood
Today we are very gentle
With each other and with the fragile shoots
That have sprung where
We splashed the snow with our cries

I am sunk oh so well deep
In love with you
That I think the stars may go out
For good if I lose again
Even for a syllable's harshness
The Eden tree that grows out
Of our eyes with its golden fruit

May we soon lay the milky comfort
Of our joined flesh over our hunger

Eureka

Turning to sponge a flank
In the bath, a new manoeuvre
Out of laziness, flue, old age,
I discover a big brown mole
That you must often have met
And wonder what else you know
Of me secret from even myself,
What other blemishes of mind
Or body you caress lovingly
Behind my back.

A Pop Up Card

Tomorrow morning birds and their mates
Will go valentining up the King's Road
In Spring feather.

I sit here trying to carve you
Entwined love knots, initials,
Would paste on my heart
But I cut it out long ago
To hang round your neck.
So there is only a verse
And a love now
As old fangled as our trinity
Or lace cunningly worked
Of sighs, desires, those love knots again,
En bon point on our pillow.
Let them seem fresh to you:
Matter for new marvel.

The dictionary tells me
There were two saints
For this date; martyrs.
They never spilled more heart's blood
Than I would to make you
Red roses out of winter's aconite.

So when you must choose, my turtle,
And the year awake,
Let me bill and build for you.
Ruffle your plumage white dove;
With you my summer sets on.

Handbook for a Bedside Table

Waiting on love the queen
leans to her ministering women
or swings airily
while the black and blue passion clouds
blossom like lovers' pinches.

'During thunder, lightning, rain
are women easily subjected
and in Spring'
I would add snow Kalyana
when both heart and flesh
swoon whitely melting
as today.

Waiting on love I flex
thews, thighs like a dancer
or boxer knowing
I will get as good as I give
have no need of a flowery mantra.

'That which is soft inside
as the filaments of the lotus flower
that is the best'
O Kalyana how could you know
who have not visited her
petalled chamber?

And the women of Guzerat
Larice, Audh, the
Coromandel country, even of
Krishna's own Mathra
with all their amorous virtues
are sluts, whores, baggages unversed
beside her.

Take your recipes of tamarind
quick silver, aniseed of gobstoppers
white panic, brute borax
and pound them into the dust

one touch of her Kalyana would make
your dead bones start
and she is all mine.

Waiting already on our next loving I
rehearse gestures, postures
of our pleasure ornate
with love's invention
our handbook Kalyana
is to lie down together.

Sometimes I am nigh you poor Clare
who were Wellington with his head shot off,
brained Nelson, Lord Juan Byron,
Bard, bruiser Spring fists doubled
against all comers,
cocky bantam in your five foot two
who should have known no more
of rhyme than chants to scare the birds,
vowed to that 'hope, love, joy',
forgetting man can't live by word alone
without bread's wholemeal crumbling on the tongue;
crazed by three witches:
the vampire muse, Mary that never was
from a boy's blush to her old maid death
and that jilt fame who kept you
for a night so you'd remember
then slammed the door at your back.

Sometimes I see you half rimed
from lying out while starlight
slugged you with frost and goblins gabbled
in the park you dared not pass
or porticoed with age under a white thatch
with an obstinate body that couldn't break
or be broken by madhouse bars
and your mind part dark, part gleaming
numbed with the night's cold

as if sent to Maxey for flour
you were faeried off the track forever
and dwell now at the twilight edge
of things, beckoning
Jack o'lantern to lovers, poets.

Yet I can't suck as you did
laudanum at Nature's promiscuous breast,
cornucopian with flowers, beespit, birdhymn
all small sharp sweets;
only her love eases me when I lie down
with the ghoul gab twittering
in my head of loss; the manmade substance
of her pink tissue in my hand
like a crumpled roseleaf
and her perfume phialed, heavy
with echo of her body's musk
charm me against marshlights
your cloudy halfmoon.

Held in her eyes I am.

EVESONG

Evesong

My love takes an apple to bed
apple, apple she puts the bite on you
or drops you, irresistible, to halt my chase.
As I pick you up and consider
your shape, texture
your virgin unblushed green
she is gone over the dream horizon
while I labour after with this
core, kore, mon cœur, half eaten
bitten fingernail of a poem
going down with the moon
these pips my teeth crack
for a taste of
bittersweet as almond skinned
cleft and dimpled
the apples she brings to bed.

Sapphic Her Dressing

My handmaidens are you going
behind that lace wicket
that keeps you close?

Are you tired of laying down
your white petals for me to tread
lifting your arms above your head
in our dance?

My three graces, all oblique angles
of your classic pose have been
my study these hours.

Now like the clouding moon
you retire to the intricacies
of woven night. Pause
there a moment.

Just once more let me
take those soft bosses in my lips
and my tongue search out
that ferny valley.

Malleus: Deposition

Late: the stars skulk in cloud
and the moon drops a pleading ray
as if for some painter to take
her up, virgin, not hunting tonight
but simply cold. I chatter
hearing your tiredness yet harsh
as if this invisible line
was a whip to lash you into
concern, demanding behind my
black plastic words impossible answers
like the thin boy who creeps upstairs
to Sylvia's room where he can
sate his hopes on highboots, mackintosh
pussy o'nine tails. Forgive me
my inconsequence, impotence
of distance which is time from you
my flashes on exhibition
like a student's first brash work
oh all my study, forgive me
best of bone and blood, your unholy
inquisitor, my slashes of red
and blue, hot scars in mortised limbs
that would hold you or have you
drop; my goads, racks, scaffolds
of love where I keep you hanging
on the mercy of my trap shut.
Forgive me for I go into
quicklime night that rots
my flesh, my trust, and if I rise
Lazarus shrouded to find you
have not called these my familiars
in my whitening sepulcre
welcome me heretic back.

For Madame Chatte

Some breasts are erectile
you say. It may be.
I can only speak of those
that are sleepy
heavy with pale dreams
awaken to my lips
pout but with maiden mouths
are marbled
hang full as swung
Parian grapes, as peaches
espaliered drowsy on a South wall
that send pleasures about her body
winged with my breath
or fuse fires from my flame tongue
that give me aery food
that are all welcome.

When we break our flesh apart
it's like tearing the petals
from Spring magnolias.
The scream is soundless
though perfection dies.

Post Impressionism

I Lautrec back on my knees
behind me can-can is going on
where you are, your metaphorical red locks
flying, your butt or leg lifted
cocks a delicate snook at irrationalities
a flamboyant link to see me home.
There I brood on angles of you at bath
dressing, or reclining abed
while I watch with hot grey matter
for sketchpad before a sharp knife
of absence etches the lines deep.
I print fourposters of you
and hack them to pieces before
the world comes staring to whistle
after you with an errand boy's unconcern.
At midnight you recline operatic
on a sofa in my head waiting for me
to key the door, untop my hat
throw myself lyric tenor at your knees.
You lift my inadequacies into a register
where no one has sung before.

To An Old Tune: Goddesses

Nerthus, he wrote, fingers out the landscape
with her shining ashfork
not hinting at the long dead
with their lips tanned back
from clenched teeth, bog bound
a noose about their necks
tumbled into sacrifice on a meal
of grain gruel to nurture the Spring.
Northern Aphrodite with your
inflexible cuntsplit take
this offering, these taut words
about my throat, the hours I marsh through
with every clinging second preserved
in formalin time. Dig me up
I shan't, I promise, crumble at the touch
of her light and air. Only raise for you
maypole in her garden where I dance
ribboned and foolscapped to bring in
another Spring, plant kisses where the fork
divides til it soften into flesh
and finger me a dreamscape
where time and our seasons never fly.

A Marvell

Oh world enough we have but lack time
next to poverty the greatest crime
world enough picking delicate among your thoughts
cultivated ways, prospects, resort
of honeycomb, rock lettered through with love
paperhats, catch me I'm yours, Venus doves
like sugar mice or gulls to loft our heart strings
bannering skyward from their wings;
enough my world to gaze, graze your pale uplands
that jewel casket opening to my hands
gold wire, twin domes of rose quartz
tipped with rubies trembling to my lips
full pendant, warm dunes of thigh
where I could bask away eternity.
    But time before our love began
had licensed half a life to run
and rings his bells and dims his light
threat'ning our lovedrunk joy with night;
lays work and wisdom to entrap
our lust and with his sunk veins sap
our livening dew, shows with each night's gash
how grave will taste our severed flesh;
my fool fresh tears that fall in vain
be indistinguishable from rain
and you who hated rural things
shall down to earth with me and kings.
    Therefore now, I would cajole
but words fall back before that dole
of smudge tired eyes and waif white face
and lust to love gives up his place.
Pleasure must honey ooze not tear
those tender gates like vultures; lie there
mistress and dream in my declining sun;
tomorrow we will make him run.

Marbles

Marbles Praxiteles carved rested chill
a millenium on the seabed with only the tide's
come and go between their thighs
the silver fingers of fish to stroke their breasts.
Smiling they let the sand embrace them
the seaworm trace his accounts on their stone flesh
weeds grow familiar with their lips and eyes.
Drawn up into daylight they are cold still
exposed to the common stare
they exude no ozone from their long sleep
no hot cockle steam from between
those sea-raped thighs that might set
monkeys aflame or men.
They move us mainly to admiration.
Laid on our seabed where I
recurrent as tides, fluid as waved weed
let my wishes shoal foraging between your thighs
you let fall ambergris to distill
the world's perfumes.

For Her Birthday

When Lleu wanted a girl they had to
make him one out of blossoms
to betray him.
They have made me one out of
peonies, white and camellias
but everlasting.
Flowers only fade on flirts.

124

Necrophilia II

Tear out my eyes.
Put them up among those dead sparklers
that tell only distance by their come and go.

Wax up my ears
so no siren sound her tongue makes
by nature hermit in my skull's carapace.

Stitch my shrunk lips.
Cobble them tight: a moist brush from hers
might bellows in the dried flatfish of my lungs.

Lead case the heart.
Her foot over my dust would tremble
it to beat, blood run, and then the dead arise.

Old men on the hard bench
at winter's edge
dribble vitriol on today
sunning themselves in childhood's afterglow
of discipline, tasks, birdsnesting
in the wood where adventure
came in cuckoopint size
when the guiltiest sweet was thieved from Woolworth's
an Easter egg that spawned hundreds-and-thousands
in eternal resurrection from its chocolate womb.
Life ever after was all declension.

Young men catnapping
on the hot hard tiles of their dreams
vivisectors out for
pet pussy in the bag moan in sleep
for the velvet vamped from memory
of a million pinups identikit
funfur to lance with their long knives
into oblivion, doubling up numbers
take away the one you first thought of
keep the tallest tail
for the one that got away.

Only I it sometimes seems
the stables mucked out
the hydra monster headed off
have brought home happiness captive
in my prime, a fate usually reserved
for gods and heroes, to stand
smiling naked in the world's eye
beat my sword into ploughshare
unhelm me, blunt my boorspear.
You tell me your name is love.

Special Relativity

Useless to pretend that time goes on
without you though outside the window
a day for lovers strolls by trailing a pale hem
our relativity, you there, me here
makes clocks run slow. Meeting I drag
a foot til we're in beat again
our bells praising the same hours.
The calculator stabs home on my nerve ends
posits a minus total, anti-number, anti-matter.
I am the timepiece sent
about the world while you stay ticking
seconds there whichever moves. I lag.
Arriving back I'm where we were
before. Spaced out I hung
weightless, colourless, time stopped.
Let me pretend that my chill earth revolves
the seasons change, birds touch
their plumage into mating suits.
Your sun comes up to warm my frozen track
day rises, glacial hours dissolve
run in droplet seconds round your feet
to carry you timeless to my barbarous shore.

Pasiphae

Cuntsmell on my hands. I have been
a bull in a porcelain shop trampling china roses
harsh and fierce when I should be kind
strutted among your thoughts
when I should have stood back
let you go into first night
where your brainchildren sang on a silver screen
have sweated and snorted when concertos
were chambering in your ears.

My head sways heavy with animal guilt
with bloodlust to run you down
hold you between my hooved forepaws
lower my curled and steaming skull
to munch among that mound of white lilies
your belly. Sweet matador, I am on my knees.
In my flanks your lances shake their pennons
the sun drinks my blood. The crowd will roar
if you lower your slim sword into my heart
and I shall have nothing further to fear.
But if you raise my head, twine flowers
between my horns I shall be ungrateful
as savages, dumb brutes and turn
to nuzzle again among the heaped
lilies of your breasts.

Easter Sonnet

Gravel on my window rains as if the day
wanted to be let in out of its own weeping cold
a northeaster flinging unaccustomed tears
at the panes I press my gaze to charging
a pigeon post in refuge on the still
to goshawk a message down the road for me.
It would show my thoughts gone out early
to a place of tombs with spices, anointment
for your desired body, pieta wrapped
away from me in the swaddling of the dead.

Or reverse the image since on feast days
our eyes mirror each other, hang me up there
to harrow hell for you so those old prophets
Catullus, Spenser, our father in love
John Donne look up surprised to see me come
trailing your lightenings, cry. 'This we foreshadowed
but never such resurrection, such despite of time.'

Host-Politick

Taste of your kisses on my lips
I lick down
as deer in winter the salt patches
the brackish tide
throws up in pans. It's easy
to rage reading
for a degree in the inhumanities
that in old age
will convert to a fellowship for mellowed
all souls. But
the clear anarchy of love won't
be reconciled
by the promise of an Indian summer.
You judge him
as he said a foolish passionate old man
fascist of the senses
muddled, muddied, yet he knew personal
over and under rides
political. Licking the saltpan of
palm, lips
underarm, cunt I renew myself
for whatever
has to be done. Dido abandoned wrecked
an empire
and she was right: there are imperatives
of the heart
that build commonweal. Without them we
concentrate
into camps, opposed, barbed. The saltpan
valley of the blaze
of light between your breasts where I know
no evil: your cup that
runneth over making me mankind
these shall be left
for patterns of society where there was
neither emperor
nor empire but two who stood up and said
this we shall do
and kissed. Deer
come down to the saltpans; we have packed
the hunters home
and this is bread in our outstretched palms.

Mythical History
Birth of a Celtic Venus

How did you come then lady
packed in with a thornbush
and dour missionary Joseph or naked
in a legionary's kit of songs
after lights out beyond the wall
but most likely coracled in an uncouth
seashell of wickerwork and skins yet
luminous to the kneeling watchers on the shore?

How did you come to me lady?
I remember a boat and driven spume
me tracking you down to where
you figureheaded in the bow and posing
with scullion insolence questions
that would dandle you my puppet
except that suddenly you pulled the string
and I have danced ever after.

Gwynhwyvar was the best they could tongue
as you stepped through the newbirth foam
saying afterwards it meant white, shining
for that was their vision while waves curliqued
back from your child's feet.
I recognize the opal of that skin
that must have dazzled their halfbeast eyes.
Not knowing what to do they wove you
a king and people while the scullion
flexed every morning before the mirror shield
and scrubbed swart muscles with milkwort
having heard somewhere, oh the ubiquity
inaccuracy of oral tradition
that you only liked adonai, a lord
became overnight a poet to scribble
your new legends and lance flying the pennon
of your white body.

Do not leave us again lady
though the island is small
not perfumed like Paphos and the climate foul
it can't sully your shining. I will give you
every day fresh dream worlds for homage
spring flowers on your altar and to nourish
blood from that grail you hold in your hands.

Early Morning Call

Struggle into porridge dark
the sleep caul still wrinkled thick
over eyes and mouth a quick wash slaps awake.
Ready aging Cherubino, now the cloak?
And the Countess? She lies soft
downed in the caress of sheets.

Getting up early is like drowning
for the shapes that rise, wrack and ammonite
seabedded deep with father's
shut oyster eyes.

At Liverpool street childhood begins and ends
eastward is only loss: a twentyfirst gold watch
bought at the jeweller's caverned in steam
above the track by special concession
squandered in a firework battle on Hampstead Heath.
Beyond the fens move out to take the city
November fields stand ankledeep in puddles
my mind trains through already
while hands brew tea, boil egg.

Young noblemen don't whine scrambling at first light
buckle on your sword. Only the conscript
drags into his baggy trousers cursing.
You go alone to duel.
The price for your smart tight pants
no unseemly frowsted dawn
with warmth of weeping doxy at your neck
though all departures are the one
from which there was no going home ever
except in dreams to find the impossible
cancelled, the return half ticket clipped.
I rinse away the dregs; crush the empty shell.
The telephone rings. Your Countess is awake
hanging your soft words furred with sleep
about my neck, shameless as any doxy
in your remembered, reminding nakedness.
I swagger into the street. Already I am half way home.

Three Latenight Sonnetinas

Chaste she sleeps in blood and tears of sweat
I would gather in the empty limbec
of my heart run dry of grief distilled away
by searing absence, common sense, it hangs
like an old hot water bottle perished
beaten flat on a stone of labour
navvied into a common shape of abstinence
as harsh, unlovely as winter chilblains.

Only for this I hug cold uncomfort
to my gooseflesh in night's rare sharp air
her breath too labours on this northface slope
that would slither us down to kingdom come
except that his thread, these paid out lines
lash us together, warp her heart to mine.

                    *

Indifferent honest I yet accuse me
of unnatural faults as of loving you
beyond rhyme or reason, of laying
the burden of me not only between
those soft thighs but deep in your eyes that hold
all my vision, my image of myself
shrunk to your pupil in love who learnt
your lesson in pleasure and can't forget

who took this untutored savage and shaped
my brute sounds to your tongue, let me gambol
aping your white limbs with my gestures
as if I had picked up a softpaste gilt cup
in my rough paw and held it with my breath
too frail a treasure against my shaggy hide.

                    *

You shall not find me Dido mercifully
false giving ear to fate or images
that would beckon me away to your rest.
While you build your city I clamour
to hold the twine for your paces

134

con the blueprints, stick my nose impertinent
between the lines, ask you a thousand times
where the theatre will be, temple and market square.

You shall not have spark for that tinder
your immortalizing pyre, I douse
all such flames with my tears, sigh out your fires
or blow them sideways where they lick through
my entrails and loins to cast that fortune
I would have divined only by my heart's steady beat.

Ride in the Dark

The wolves are out tonight
their knobbed snouts glisten
wet pontefract cakes by moon
howl down our silence.

Faster I crack the thongs
over my sweating haunches
the runners steel slice our track
hot knives through butter.

Bat branches swoop churchyard
black; flaying evergreen
needles my cheeks; the wolves' breath
reeks musty as butcher's sawdust.

I would drop rein, crouch, whimper
in the snow but I hear
you sing clearer than bells behind me
where you ride muffed against cold and dark.

The gates of the green palace blaze open
a jewelled reliquary to flesh our bones of love.
Beneath the silk strands of your song
charmed the wolves drop back.

As to the wars
impressed by the bloody corporal
circumstance I up and go
his henchman time carbine cocked
against my naked breast
no argument. I must serve out
the heaving tides' best
the trenches' worst.
Adrift on the night
as eyebrows icicle with unwilling breath
uneasy come and go
the body's heat drops to the falling dark
of polar winter, a world away from you.
Towards the angling sun
subarctic carrying on
glazed broody phoenixes of my hope
ridiculous in morning dress
the penguin fathers about turn
my golden eggs between their webbed galoshes
heavy with fledgling dawn.
All agonies are two thirds deep
in bitter water and the fireworked
night wheels spiteful
with mockery of splendour
like bombardment
where I cringe in a shellhole
muddied, rotten with tears
mine, awaiting the soft lead
with my name cut deep
that will nose a blunt way into my heart.

Good night I flatter
cover me. That she is there
I here is so monstrous
a civil war, pressgang
that rips the lover untimely
from his mistress' belly
for the night queen death's shilling
that I cannot see how
the candle stars prick on

136

in my eyes or the poles
not melt and run together.
Going I beg a kiss longer
lest the first incision
should sever my heart's blood's channel
and it pump out in knotting gouts
like those roses, another
and again to deaden
the amputation while she would be
off quick. Sorrow you are not
sweet as at their first parting
trifle of sugarplums and green angelica love.
You are cascara making the gut
cloacine well with fear
and loss. You are the heavy tread
on the stair, the punishment
for being too old, too young
drunk one night before she was
and swearing for oblivion
for all weakness
for five foot five
for myself
unwilling recruit this night
in an outpost of watching.

Villonelle

Yesterday's darlings, dear dames, demoiselles
all dead delights that were or never
time took from you to weave my mistress fair.

Some in the mind's eye canvassed by painters
others noted, breathed into comely song
yesterday's darlings, dear dames, demoiselles.

For exhortation of virgins a saint's swoon
for comfort of sinners a magdalen tear
time took from you to weave my mistress fair

the breast of Venus in galactic birth
Boudicca's rage, Flos Campi, Portia's tongue.
Yesterday's darlings, dear dames, demoiselles

have no marvel that I do her service
who is more than the sum of those blended wonders
time took from you to weave my mistress fair.

You too shall be worshipped, piecemeal but wholly
with here my mind, there my mouth, reincarnate
yesterday's darlings, dear dames, demoiselles
time took from to weave my mistress fair.

Cupid and Psyche

Mourning we become children
wanting to put back clocks
reverse time's order of events
an agenda we can't rewrite.

At our perennial private
meeting we rehearse balances
we can only make by throwing
love deadpan into the light scale.

Annually this time of birthday
we murder our first loves
relive the moment we weren't there
heap guilts like Psyche's seeds to sort.

Yet love in at your window
I thrust my counterpoise.
If you will endure, unscramble
crosswords of againstgrains piled

I will pour my hot oil on
troubling waters though it burn
my heart's flesh and tell you close
the casement on the beckoning dark.

My childhood was given to dying
it was as commonplace as tomorrow
but would come. I don't remember
a time when the death's head
over the shoulder wasn't neighbourly
not mine own at first but love's death
and so mine.

As I grew it was turned to a desperate
living, adolescence was into future
for the present held nothing worth keeping
and maturity's song was sickly with maybe tomorrow.
Death, I said, hold off til I live.

Now my hair whitening round old bones
fissures widening under my eyes
he looks again over my shoulder.
I bargain: five years of mine
for one day of her fears.
More then. How much to make her laugh?
Take it. And if you come
beckoning her into some autumn evening
of mist and bonefires, at the crossroads
where the light falls straight
you will find my features
flower under your green fingers.

Actaeon

As if I might a summer god drop down
here on the winter's edge, the thicket
dense with spears, fall to my knees
while you or my own lusting hounds
sever my throat already seamed
with the horns branched weight
candelabra to your aim
forcing my head low, eyes abased
tendering my own flesh
November fogs my tongue.

No need to chase or fly:
one step from the pool's rim
your body drawn away behind
cloaks of attendant hair and suckerwhite arms
I stumble, my feet and hands
hooving, cleft and hard as nails
party to my own cull.
Cut me out. I am weak with love
will never see snow through
to the moss and black goodless turf.

I scrape at bark only to incise
your name on growing wood
and as frost rimes in the groves
incense my swung breath with prayers
for your indifferent hand that wouldn't
put me down. Cheeky was I
to look and want such limned perfection
and your slither downbank towards me
through the mirror pool
a lapse I should die for.

Loose your arrow.
This rough pelt can't hide
you from my sight or wind down
those hounding cries.

Journey to Cythera
'Ile des doux secrets et des fêtes du coeur!'

Voyage Out

In the mind's eye the island lies
just off centre to be come at
by prayer, work, faithfulness rewarded
is no commonplace of geography
but needs stargazing, a commitment
to the deep, is Circe's isle
where men could be pigs by failure
of dreams or might Ulysses storm
all ramparts to be gods; just off
the motorway wherever you pitch
in an oasis of flight up the unfurling tarmac.
At the desk they will give you keys
to open all doors to burgle pleasure
rifle sweets; hot towels and soft water
whatever the emir wanted for sherbet
silk hangings; electronic zithers.
Among damp green dunes, mists
you loom suddenly Cythera.

Invocation

All arms are laid aside
naked we lie. You have a cold
and grampus through sleep. My belly aches
from strange food and hunching over the wheel.
Mortality challenges with a struck shield.
It takes time to cure the itch of everyday
and time ends in the skullmouth's
hic iacet. Time is the mist that laps
the island, obscuring, eroding
the innocent shores of pleasure.
Immortal Cythera touch us into eternity.

The Shrine

One traveller whose barque grounded
on the shingle saw the shrine a gibbet
with himself adangle, breathed an air
rancid with his own vomit; another
the goddess terminal, her embrace broken
her garlands faded paper roses
we find only what we take to altars.
I make my temple out of your living
flesh and the beasts that romp guard
about you, my gentle lusts, are
tamed to your service tigers.
The dark thickets glow at the island's heart
as I come home, rock in your bay
and hear the shell singing of your siren cries.
Thin walls have ears to pick up our pleasure.
Let them envy whose swartsailed ships
never found your latitudes Cythera.

The Bay

In season the bay is pebbled thick
with patina of laced bodies, families picnic
sandwich between pulls at the sea
spindle legs urchin and starfish
in the shoals. Chipshops batter
the air with hot fry, care goes down
a third time in the boozy foam
barbirds summerplumaged mew and chatter.
Today there is only water and pale soft sand
planes of gliding light to dazzle our mused eyes.
You strew your late roses from hedged gardens
Cythera, like baskets of petals beneath our wheels.

The Return

Loves swarm the rigging for the journey back
ladders of threaded beams let down on flowing land
unleaving autumn masts, greengilt canvas
flushed with the year's sunset are their playground.

Lover look back; imprint this image
on the heart's retina that in icetime
dulled with winterlabour you may conjure
again with touch and murmur
these days' smiling langour.

There is no departure:
where she is the island rises shining
and your white shores are her breasts and thighs Cythera.

Seen through your eyes I am nine feet tall
and yet so small I might creep
into your acorn cup, flower
maidenhead.

Seen in your eyes made baby
Tom Thumb, cupid caressed
I am part of you perfected
in those mirrors

with no need to shy from shop windows
the refractory glasses
of others' stares, my own reflected
nakedness.

Old circumscriptions no longer bleed.
Become your frog prince, the answer
to my child question: 'Ugly as a toad
I would still

love you,' sinks resolved. Yourself
seen in my eyes wide with the curving
planes of you, all my land of milk
and honey

do you not recognize you too
beautiful, queen, all-homaged
brilliant in resurrection? Be seen
through my eyes.

On Rubens' Garden of Love *at Waddesdon Manor*

This face and this; his, hers
here everwhere, lips meeting
heads reclined and hands in touch
a figure leaning back to take in love
a bloom of half blushed flesh
did she cry then
the veil first flung back from the easel stare
catching a soft hand to her rich white breast
moth at a sleepy scented pale corolla
as you do now
no not me?

If she could have seen her now
for all eyes to fall on
at a fee
(parrots scream in the gardens
in livery of red and green
polling the chestnuts, billing in the oak)
ripe bourgeoise, could she have known
their loves would have been
common property
painted zoo and aviary of turtle dove
poor man's pornography
would she have cried
not me?

My stroke trembles:
however close I run
our last lust down
or pick your perfection out in
beds of blossoming, praise in truth
the least gesture's subtle music
on my skin stretched taut
to your every touch
at the passover words, when I drop
my everyday lenten array for resurrection
of your perfect and my raised flesh
you say to Magdalen lines
no not me.

Breakdown

All perishing afternoon you have sat in the bleak
of an endless motorway that leads nowhere as yet
though one day they say it will be gloriously
gone West, sundown at Camelot riding into the sea
now it takes fright at the green belt hitching up
London and turns back on itself. Today it is alien
as arctic, watermarking the tarmac with rimy
flurries where polar bears might lumber snowsalted
furred at the edges hallucinatory against the grey
pelt of the sky whose swag lies heavy on taut March
earth and buds and birds regret their Valentining
forwardness, their half feathered nests and bloody
rose shoots. You have sat with a pain in the belly
uncomplaining while my, I accept all responsibility
starter hemmed phlegmatic like an old man's morning
and died. You have supped a liquor sweet and acid
at once like sick who should always be champagned
listening half to me chatter nervous as the bird
we spotted out of the window grey wagging its tail
artificial as the emperor's nightingale or
the clockwork Leopold Mozart toy symphonied for
pecking at what seemed nothing on the gravel court.
This wasn't how I planned the afternoon.
Finally I got you to empurpled sheets
spread earlier clean and royal for seduction
yes, even after four years, and we lay
wrapped in each other, iglooed against the motorway
that goes nowhere, flaying winds that would slice us
into pemmican to be chewed slowly in a long night.
Spring that deceive and plugs that won't spark
where we made not fierce summer but October
soft light lit by flashes I recognize as
aurora borealis, a yeartime of loving
out of a fled, raw afternoon.

The Pinefoam Bath

Lapped she luxuriates, lies
a grained marble strand in turquoise seas
or moonstone in chrysoprase bed
while spices and herbs nudge her flesh
with their pertinent scents, essences
poured out or bruised in her service
as if she were some greek theatre
white moulded on the hillside
where wild thyme crushes sage underfoot
and all my desires act out in the sun's eye.
Bold waves plant cairns of bubbles on those
slopes to boast they were there or drop
seed pearls in the valley between her thighs
where I snubnosed dolphin might bask
or founder drowned lashing my tail
and diving deeper than these mild spawn
I should not envy. All siren beauty
singing alone on a barred shore is cruel.

My reassurances syrup down the phone
splashback hot drops on my skin like tears
unlucky in cards I try to build a sheltering
roof lodged on a hope, socketed to fear
joker or ace or two impertinent jacks
giant-killer, beanstalk-climber, clowns
playing loamcast walls that will cardhouse down
with the first breath of dark, both me and I.

I beg you hold me who am slippery
as dreams, fancy's elf, Theresa's angel
or demon insubstantial who pierces
but leaves no stigmata, no signature
in the willing flesh but crouches apart wondering if
cries go home, if will can seed an inkling in your heart.

Therapy

Keep on, they said, you'll find the lady there
by the swart rocks, lashed to a punishing stake.
Tighten your helm, the dragon spews out fire.
We'll leave you here; a tempest's coming up.
The prints of clouds bruise the midday sky.
His horse plods plashily, smudging the sand ribs
where girls might bathe naked in midnight velvet
pulling the foam over phosperescent breasts.

Beyond the promontory, her people said.
He hefts his lance and loosens out his sword.
Just past these rocks and he must see her soon;
a lady leading on a silken leash
a lizard shape that dances in her wake
ripples its coils whose soaring verey lights
dazzle her eyes. Each day she walks it
trims its horns with bladderwrack, shines its scales.

Where's that nakedness, the pinioned bait?
Her eyes look up to spill at his approach
knowing he brings death and desire
pacing the shore, scuttling thwarted crabs.
The animal flower anemones blob
as his coarse hoofs tremble the rock pools.
Better the dragon she knows than this
that would lead her from her stranded games

the beckon of waves, perfection of despair
to the mortality of love.
What should he do; throw his spear
far out in the gulfing waves?
Drop his reins and let her lead him too
about the sands quicksilver with death
or thrust through that gambolling mainspring snake
and chance breaking her heart?

Nowell

This winter baby garners
all the toys: his, hers
gobbles a Christmas turkey, cuckoos the nest.
Limelight and praise he hogs.
From his warm manger dogs
us with guilt for his no-room-inn, outcast
birth while he lies chuckling hero
among bowed beasts' breaths patient come and go

He whored his mother
young Oedipus, was father
to his sonship with piercing angel words
had her his handmaid
a fresh mild virgin laid
sacrifice to his thrust like all Nowell birds
trussed, forcemeat stuffed. He bastes her thighs
with sweated labour; his first hymns her cries.

Before we were he came
his aureole of flame
casts into shade our nursery nightlight glow
and every year brings round
heraldic horns that sound
his newborn praise across the maiden snow
the clockwork kings set forth
perfume and gold proclaim his ambisexual worth.

Even the rough shepherds
flock down the mountain roads
sheep shouldered, hard hands laid to monarchist hearts
while we outherod swords
cut throats and tighten cords
massacre could-be siblings with our darts
hurry him into Egypt's sand
exile him from our royal murdering hand.

I could forgive him all.
Loved bastard, at my call
the world ran, bent, smiled, heaped gilded phials
but at the bedgrave's foot

150

you weep in childish guilt
for the Santa'd pillowcase bulging ills
heavy upon your threeyear head
lie the strewn presents, too much your tears said.

Let me be pastor
lead the whiteflocked dreams your
age allows back to the cradle, wipe your eyes
dispossess that prince
who took your infant peace
dandle and hymn you, with my rough pipe disguise
all minor keys till you laugh enough
gathering my bounty to you with a lover's touch.

Mon Semblable, Mon Frere

Caliban silhouetted King Kong against the sunset
your headland, this isle
tonight is full of noises
sounds and sweet airs
that are her voices
and those twangled instruments your heartstrings
hum round your ears to make you dream again.
You stockfish, walking codpiece, bouille-baisse
one extra s curled like a whiting or wanton eel
puts down from kiss to curse
clown pickled herring in a brine of tears and sack
would have peopled all your realm
with monsterlings got on that wonder
as she schooled your oceans of ignorance
would have scaled, topped and tailed
her beauty. If you could have kept her
away from all brave new worlds
that had such lovers in them
you would have chopped wood like any prince
brought water, fruits, milk, cheese
a pastoral to delight her
made her mermaid but her swart father
in enchanting starsewn cloak shipwrecked
a soft boy to her shore
and sailed them both away.
Don't think had the gales been right
you couldn't have coracled her
to some lagoon where his ariel spirit
couldn't pinch your innocent lusting flesh
or that she won't in her castle
sigh sometimes for your wrack
flotsam of desire's high tide
over her threshold, starfish
pirate cuttlebone, scoured glass opaque with
its message while you trace
as she taught you, her name
at the sea's mouth, the marvel
time and tide waver to devour.
In the morning you can play Ferdinand
and prince it on her stair.

Bottom's Song

About this wood: let me tell you
before I came here I was all kinds of fool
playing at passion, rehearsing tragedies

a braggadoccio figure of fun
I clowned high seriousness watching myself
lofting on half formed nibs, from the wings

but here I was cast in a new role.
My ear burned; some one was gossiping about me
left my lover or was it only the new furred coat

my many coloured mistress threw around me
made me seem suddenly Midas touched
could turn my dreams to gold I whispered to the reeds.

What I have been here I can't tell you
or what she did but all my defects, doltish
perceptions were twined in blossoms, perfumed

made much of so that I could command
the weathers, am a king breaking all bounds
of time, place, sing and her ears listen as to seashells.

Not for Duke, dukedoms or sixpence
a day will I lose my asshead; let none take
from her eyes that blindness that makes this fool wise.

'Look to the Lady'
(Pericles)

Your head now castaway
on its pillow Thaisa
shut in the seachest coffin
of sleep, bears you tranced
through tempests, tossed
while the fishes and monsters
of the deep come peer at you.
Between death and life waiting
some necromancy of love
to quicken those my limbs
I committed alone to the waves
you sail out my long watch
at mercy of tides and winds
whitecaps and Neptune who would
sprat spit you on his toasting fork
a salt morsel to his taste.
Behind your closed eyes sea horses
canter, Leviathan swallows his tail
fishmaids sport. Your waking vows
you to Diana while I adrift too
shift out the moons and ebb
and flow til morning. I have forgot
myself. I was a prince once
don't laugh, by virtue of my sovranty
over a fair piece of earth I could span
with my body and was let walk in
by election. Spin me briny yarns
of your dreams. Deciphering
the prints of night birds in sand
by the lie of spar, clouded glass
bladder wrack I foretell
at high tideline my own voyage home.

Meetings
after Veronese

The family of Darius have come out
weeping, sinking to their knees.
Do not rape us, do not send the sharp swords
through our bodies, while he says
I am not the man you think
steps back pointing like a dog at taken game
where he is emperor, conqueror.
I am only his henchman
make suit to him.

Does it teach us how to behave
this picture? Did he raise this lady
on his swordpoint glance and lay her down
in spite of her grief, his henchman
armies, that Persian or blackface
in the background?

You come up the road to me
sink into a chair and say:
Well, do you want to go to bed
in spite of tiredness and I am
at once conqueror, emperor
permitted to sheath my sword in you
make my own laws, a Hammurabi
say this your limbs will do and this
or you incur my greatest penalty
which is to die at once under my stroke.

Does he become the lover of that queen?
There are her caryatid daughters
nubile but legend says she
made the barbarian fit emperor. Therefore they are
for this painted moment held as she kneels
as if someone had caught us
you touched down half an hour before
coming towards me across a day's waiting
(West London terminal we have made you
immortal) and your face showing
the conquest of time I ratified
this afternoon in your arms
when we both behaved beautifully.

The Historians and Helen

The whole affair was just a trick of trade
Paris not prince of course
but merchant chief.
Achilles, Patroclus two
banking firms; his rage
takeover bid; his death a crash.
Interests can be repaired
but limbs go cold, they rot.
Lust, or was it love, might fade
the seamen watching as he sailed her home
sniggered a dirty joke Yeats didn't hear.
Girls were for treaties
their bodies lands, alliances
rape one, you cornered
vineyards and goldsmiths
jars of oil and wine
to pour in fleshly wounds.

But what if it wasn't like that
if out of rumours, the trash of
the local press Homer made
picking among his lyre strings
heartstrings, a fiction
the facts layer out in burnt towns
shards, a fragment of amber?
What if he only made us
prototype geometric of mistress and lover
didn't he make history?

Pornopack

This morning through the post a time bomb
hair triggered by the torn envelope
lacerating the soft gut with splinters of hate
unexpected as Borgiaed wine therefore deathly
an obscene photograph with anonymous message
poison flower palmed off in a lilac wrapping
equating my red lust and political colour
in a monstrous malediction of a wound
held out in the vampire claws
selfpriesting for magnification.
I gather up my tumbled mumbled
shambled viscera and stuff them back.

They would have me believe the poised, paid dolls
under the infra lamp are us the bloodied lintel
my happy home Hierusalem
never in this print to be come at
in travesty of barriers unmanned
thrown down no silent peak
or far vision of crusaded holyland
that can't be bought doesn't fade
no Do Well and Have Well that isn't
clouted by a half lettered stave
to read we shall never attain kingdom-come.
I answer we have been there where gilded lilies
are sewn symbols of innocence
on a white and blue chequered ground
and saint and angel climb together the body's ladder
of perfection the tenhour bill
lights bonfires in our dancing thighs
while whores and doffers minuet free in the marketplace
and overtime is the rate for being alive.

157

Rejection Slip

Critics don't like it that my words come round
to praise. After andante the needle hops
into the unforgivable (by the bourgeois
Sartre said) hey presto happy ending
with knees up Mother Brown.
MacDiarmid had to wait three score and ten
before they would hear the hymns
through his dialectic.
Jewish I could joke: I should live so long
or black I might fit myself to an inky blues
but blitzkreig and depression stamped my genes
in a pattern for carrying on

and besides
there you are.

Advertisement for Myself

The au père boy would swagger in your dreams
nimble and deft with dishes, to run your errands
cook up your succulent commands
would scullion about your table
brown my flesh even on a spit of sunlight
for your pleasure, in a reek of prophylactic
aphrodisiac alchemy of garlic and asphodel
dish you up a dozen countries, stitch
your shouldertraps, a jacktar knotting
rigging to hold the full bosom of your sail
against cold blast Boreas, midwife you
through labours, chariot you as ripe
careful as winged Daedelus who made it
forsaking labyrinths and the pride of sun
the blizzard snowplumes and heartmelting wax
leave fun on two wheels to Phaeton, Jehu
would be grateful for any position
adaptable, conscientious, seeks overtime
has the language at tonguetip and for wages
asks only to make your bed and lie in it.

Discrimination

My negro spine curves out to end in butt
myths an 's' for sexy; swaybacked the polite term
steapygous. Look the word up: it yields
aboriginal cave paintings, signalling
we were here as long ago as the straight backs
and underdeveloped countries. Did all our fatstock
go into this, Satchmo shassey of buttock
against the world, blued putto bottom
upthrusting urchin, a dog saying arseholes
with a long stretch fore and aft? I watch myself
in shop windows going by, duck flights cocked
milord mallard and pray you will take me
for the real, royal, imperious thing.
Some countries consider it beautiful.

Carole King: Tapestry

Through the nextdoor wall music molasses
sienna sounds, umbrous in a low female register.
Why call it blues this brown study?
After the colour of overalls, chanteys to bib
and brace you against the cottonpicking sun
that would teazle your brain to a flyaway white boll
or blue gauze draped from the drift
of a thousand drags in a basement that only knows
nightlight, tattered banner to a solo muted horn?

Neighbourly the music nudges the dark
with its tale of love gone.
In answer I set spinning our harmony
with a juggler's dexterity of whirling dreams.
They say poems should lie heavy as sad cake
the fruit all gone to the bottom
that my lyrics of our pleasure float
airy spongepuffs for ballooning commercials
that all lovenotes are bluenotes. I paint
our cries purple to pin on a pink sky.
Let us make fanfares; dun songs are for
the poor in heart.

Still Room

Scent is what hunts hound after
the droppings of terror

perfume the crumble of cassia
from the mummy's wrapper

Phul-nana invested the gilt paper
Californian Poppy the unwashed ear

but Ashes of Roses, Woolworth's attar
Horatian and careless cavalier

pot pourri of burnt out desire
did we feel after you or discover

by our nostrils' censing the bitter
reek of your destroyed summer

vulgar perfume, choice scent or neither
merely our first fall to consumer?

Tonight she beats me with a fresh invader
the flower drum song of a conqueror

the cheap tarts with the dabs of scent retire
disordered into the night. Perfumed, turn over.

Dusky Windows

Other people's lives I voyeur
as we live back to back across this muse:
a boy oriental leans from a three storey frame
singlet white in the evening heat
a shirt swings sleeveless in its window breeze
someone stirs a pot in the multi-coloured kitchen
someone sheds clothes for a bath
Piero baptism candidate pulling a shirt over his head.
Out of a window along the leads
another climbs to a lighted room
while Mimi and Rudolf pour their lovenotes
from my cheap radio into the summer air.

She coughs a little. I know she will die
yet with Rudolf I'll disbelieve.
The bather draws pants and clean shirt
over the rippled undersea body
a head silhouettes as if watching me scribble
or listening; face and arm pearl grey
at a charcoal window frame.
I can stop the audience clapping if I switch off
but after there's a programme will tell us
scientifically how our blood runs
why the boy climbs eighty feet above ground
out of the window, why Rudolf weeps
why I sit here linking those lives with ours
those bohemiens, why larvae become butterfly
why the yam yields contraceptive steriods
why bananas ripen gassed in the hold
salmon home leaping from salt through sweet water
the tit turns on to feed the child.

Opposite lives grow dark as the moon swings up
or neon against the blank black walls.
Two heads align on my envy. Is it wrong
to watch lovers in and out those dusky windows
and long for you?

Sonnet

Afterwards there are dogends in the ashtray
sheets heavy with her perfume and our sweat
I don't want to change, rumpled, a curled
about her attitude I imitate in sleep
the smell of her on my skin, a towel awry
in the bathroom, the floor clouded with talcum
with careful intaglio of two footprints
all patched on this translucent autumn weather
and its Veronese foliage, each leaf
outlined and brushed with decay I interpret
as longing for a mythical landscape
all my fallacies are pathetic.

Sometimes I think I live only in my head
where she walks in a Golden Age I echo
with this lead shadow when we day after
day made consort of each other's smiles.
Yet I know it is just that those four
her hours were swift as Indian summer
this now has winter's black and measured tread.

MEMORIALS OF THE QUICK AND THE DEAD

Memorials of the Dead of Ireland

As I get older I respect the living more
even those that tend themselves like lawns
circumspect with the mower, harsh on plantain
but soft for the buttercup, the daisychain
dressing with fine sand to keep the moss at bay
their sluggish bodies on the tourist beach
snailtracked with suntan oil's viscous sheen
abrading the warm plump flesh with seasalt
sunstroke, swigging from the blue sky chalice
warm wine and lacing the skin with tidemarks
where siesta lust ran out at every pore
before home to winter, wellingtons
the snivelling days.
               The dead don't dance
though the dying sometimes sauté a last fling
the hanging man cuts a leg on air
as the warm seed slime jerks free, a last sowing
for windows to dip their handkerchiefs in
make his bequest to the frozen spermbank
and cheat death with postumous conceivings.
Only in dreams the dead take our hands to quickstep
ghoststep, obedient to their music or
in the mind's eye death himself comes leading
the round dance, palm coldsweat glued to palm
tinker, tailor, gypsy, queen, all gone
pied pipered inevitably into the hill
and the door shut fast, turfed over, a stone
to hold them down.
              These books chronicle the stones.
You cannot talk of the dead except you
saga their living: births, marriages
honours, glory in the field, all chiselled out
under the soft weeping sky: memorials
of the dead of Ireland. Mick and Prod
the pages calender them side by side
knowing they lived the same death from their cradles
suckled the same sour way, these telltale deadmen
whose genes find end in me.
             Last winter shrilled
through a gap in the window where the vent
had rusted and dropped, a chill arsehole
I have to stop before another December.

The windowcleaner fits a windmill
of pureplastic that whirls weathercock
like the kaleidoscope propellers
children run with. This flings crystal flashes
as the sun twirls in its bargain prayerwheel.
It is Shelley's white eternity I move
towards leaving the coloured windmills of childhood
stacked neatly for other hands to baton on.
At night if I pull the right string the wheel
whirls against the stars as if it might
funnel their music or their chill regard
into the kitchen reminding me I
shall soon enough be there, unheralded
remote. I can't quite be shot of my ancestry.
Death runs in the veins of the mind most
its lesions, fluxes numbing the living world.
It is the walking need our pity, an arm
under the elbow. Only live flesh bruises
spins yellow and blue, green and royal purple
webs that fade as the cells restore, ant life
putting the heap to rights. Picked bone is clean
china white with the gentility of the crooked
little finger, incorruptible in moonlight.
I pull the string and let the blades fall blank.

                              *

That year that was all funerals I have blotted out.
The loved and the unloving became ash.
They moved to banal music down into the flames
in a ritual as old as humankind
that had all meaning and none. What did they chant
the men who funnelled the charrings into urns
and sank them under posts, in cemeteries
beyond the walls of towns so they wouldn't walk
on their breaking flesh manure plague in the streets.
There's a rosebush you're memorialized by
in a garden of the planted dead where
you're scattered as you used to make a liquor
out of your dead dogends for the tobacco plants
that let fall such fragrance as we came up
rubbing our eyes from the tomb shelter
at dawn when the magic was being alive.
Memorials stand for those who never knew

to read, an advertisement to children.
'Keep off. You're green. Here's memory in rosebuds.'
Wherever you were you're there, not under
tagged stone or bush. I can make you walk
so easily I slam the door on those dreams
knowing you wouldn't have wanted to be
so remembered, would have felt it indecent.
You knew someone would shape metal on the wheel
you let stand still, plants would park their shoots
in the potting shed we built of old wardrobes
in the back bedroom and carried down.
There's no way out of our dead except love
and that death I shun as long as I can.

*

How do they find the spot in the garden
Where the small furred corpse juts stiff legs that couldn't
outrun death, stained glass blue and greenbottle
droning in the pale morning sun, busy
at decay and propagation my spade
chops short burying quickening and dead
at once. A car got you. You brought
your bloody mouth in under the briar rose
to grin into nothing. You should teach us
to be careful. But we're like you: slink
between the wheels, think ourselves charmed, hear
the beckon of the far side, set out.
And if we end under the thorns in the dust
carrion prey was it worse than never
crossing the tarmac river? As I tamp down
your flirting tail my grave's too strait a bed for
I vindicate only the frayed liberty
we wish ourselves wearing the pied clown's
trousers, harlequin blue and green that may
resurrect, take wing out of your earth
brave til the last moment perhaps then glad
like you of a briar to die under
and moist lawn to put our bloody lips to
for a last sip on life.
                    If we had never
lived it had never been. It takes its whiteness
from blended hues that run together
to death's sharp point that would seem apex
unless you read time backwards to where

a child takes a coloured streamer to dance.
We march down time bannering grey hairs
drawn teeth, blotch freckled hands. Theology
can only teach abandonment of this spoiled flesh
that semaphores the grave with its tattered flags
as if what time destroyed had never been
no dead hero or beauty ever walked
between doomed elms a bug sucks to shrivelled leaf
and the green pennants never signalled in
fifty springs.
              Outside the afternoon weeps.
The shelved pages are fretted to dust, foxed.
These died long ago yet are still dying
in unseemly lust running at the old hag
with a bullet between their teeth they plucked
out of the air or cut from mother's flesh
dying to dissolve to dust or angels
and their blood water roses. Live flesh has blooms too
flowerings of love and the kaleidoscope eyes
that see enchanted patterns. All done
by mirrors perhaps. In the glass my face
looks back mortal. Only out of your eyes
it smiles forever.
              We are still afraid
of the dark, children crying for the door
to be left open, a last drink of water
we invent heaven to put off that sleep.
Golden hierarchies lead us up by feathered
steps pillowy or incarnate lusts tailed
three-toed claw down to hell which is better
than nothing until the vision becomes
stronger than everyday. Pilgrim shoulders
his pack for the blessed fields while poor flesh
weeps and cuts its wrists with the pain of living.
Who will make pads out of the torn leaves
of tracts to stop the bleeding?
                          And you
the hirers and hirelings who filch the honey
so that our hive starves in winter until
you drive the last thin spit of beesting
to lash you to death and our queen to lay
only warrior eggs born with spears in their tails
no furry satchels on their shins for nectar
but glinting carapaces for thighs

where the silk dust that sets the next Spring
in motion can't cling, you are deathmongers
though you pad your own bones against a fall
turn down righteous thumbs on the driven
putting guns into their hands and crooking
their fingers about the trigger, pointing them
gently at their own heads. You are the wastemakers
who cuisine out of the spatter of blood
and brains the gruel to keep alive in death
of impotence, rage, calentures that suck
us down to a morning after condom
wrinkled in the gutter.
                                    Amid the tears
it has to be remembered that the man
shot and coffined in the boot of the car
was a wastemaker while the one who pulled
the trigger may have wept at nights
for the breadless child where bread is mindfood
manna the educators drop down or free milk.
It used to be warm and half gone off, the crated
bottles always stacked by the radiators
that issue of paperstraw and a third squat
of a pint that was meant to put flesh back
on soft bones, build teeth and nails broken
by a century of neglect. We poured it
down the sink after the codliver oil
the priviledged damned few of us whose cards
showed we were less than perfect, were prescribed
to patch up poverty's diseases. I am
fortyfour, older than my mother
would have believed possible who died
two years short. I know now she died young.
Possibility leers human out of mirrors.
There were still things she might do: not old enough
to be prime minister, might have made
some junior post, secretary to a man
going places except that she ran
a needle through her finger treadling up skirts.
We too have our archipelagoes reach back
far years enough. She rang as she sewed
in a register that wavered from cough to spit.
Our wire, our commandant was the friendly grocer
with no more on the slate. He had to eat too.

*

There's a society for my Irish dead
or was, that ransacks tombstones, puts all down
indiscriminately and that's right, murdered and
murderer, bandit Tory and loyalist
together. They rub spined shoulders as scapulae
stripped vertebrae will one day when their earth
is choked with dead, rub, buttress, fit sharp
buttock to dry lap until they erode
bone against sere bone and none can tell meal
from white meal. Were they meant to do just this
these volumes? Did someone have the vision
of all these dead lying down together
or standing up for man's kindsake? Elsewhere
the living stand up to be counted
but that's no substance for Fenian saga
they loved and they lived.
Grainne's girls grow up with guns in their fists
while I jot down these lifenotes, celebrations
of another country where we can make
a child's swing for long summer evenings
out of the gallowswood on the hill
where dreams can ride higher and higher
make us memorials of our loving flesh.
As I write I hear the toc toc tac
of a man in the night flaking tombstones
or putting the roof to rights.

172

On the London Poetry Secretariat Poets Card

This card says I bleed
inwardly
this card says I have been treated
and there is nothing to be done for me
this card says I work
in the sewers of the human psyche
underground
that I rat
sharp toothed on what I see among my fellows
that I burrow in the sludge
to turn up dropped watches
pearls that are your eyes
it says I am high on every kind
of unnatural hallucinogen
will make cause of the commonplace
am liable to sudden collapse
in which case they must send for her
whose touch makes new and whole.
This card says there are certain things it's no good
giving me
or they poison my system
(maybe I've had enough)
like prevarication, procrastination
that make me throw up.
This card says that vital bits of me
portative organs will still be available
for service when I'm dead
such as affirmations, celebrations
voluntaries, aires to a loved ground
like this.
This card says I am a poet
I carry it with me everywhere.

A Letter to Whom it Doesn't Concern

Pensionerwise I try to live on ten pounds a week
after rent of coursé, bubble my own wine
out of whatever's cheap in season, don't smoke
lack tele, stereo, stolen two years ago
and never capital enough to replace
back to student's monodansette
and there's my story.
England, my England don't you care
if Shakespeare's child's children beg
as long as the coaches roll in to
Stratford on Avon. We can all sleep
in the second best bed of where
herded together in Sally's arms
muttering among the meths drinkers
wild prophetic Blakean words
as long as we don't disturb you
with the truth or our wants.

Big Daddy, the foreigner, claps
his muse in asylum or campus.
Mother England has left her brood
beside the track and gone away.
Do you want us to fall onto the last circle line?
Is that it? They call that green eye
the home signal. Do you want us to take
each other's hands and jump?

Tree Fall

The saw rasps the morning into logs
that chart a tree's slow foundering
sinking to a barky knee, a marooned stump
island in the woven green lawn.
Its head of mermaid hair drops, jerks on a hangman rope
its spread arms own gallows fork the clear sky
where the young executioner swings Tarzan
though the urban jungle, silhouetted
in stark bravado every window fills
to watch, admire up there mid-July
half naked in a sudden sunburst
as the top bows to his overgrown powerdrill
we tame at home to trim the prunus
that burgeons white hopes in the Spring.
Blinded by sun moths stagger drunk with sleep
from their doomed leaf beds. Silent in the ripped air
predator thrush and blackbird let them go.
This was a false acacia, immigrant
a locust tree, John Baptist fed on
with honey for desert breakfast, native
from the New World three hundred years ago.
The tree fellers prise its spread fingers
from their grip on the earth.
I take up a slice of trunk fallen to the ground
its sunshield kept bare of other life
as the ash drips its poison onto the soil
at its feet, an invisible wall
that moats and guards it round.
My slice shows annuities: late spring, drought, flood
mapped in its rings, graphed so fine my naked eye
can't tell them round. Maybe this morning
has shipwrecked two centuries and Mozart
is playing at the inmost ring. From Cologne bridge
you can see beyond mythical Christpoint
back to when we were children of the wood spirits
and knew what we did when we cut down trees.
See that ringed jetty? Its timbers plot
where the ships tied up with oil, gods
wine, cooking pots, the centuries before the axe.
I hold an ache, oak corn in my palm.
The earth will make it a chronometer
and I can only guess at the time it will
tick over when the lasersaw brings it down.

Dead Elms Oxfordshire

At first you don't see, eyes on the road
or flicking to hobbledehoy lambs' gambol
horse nuzzle (the animals are all signed up
for card or calendar), then suddenly
the boneyard as if elephants
had come here to shuck their grey skins
in death leaving tusks erect and gristle strung
rib cage mounted or a seabottom cemetery
of the foundered with their masts
pit propping the sky above a sargasso
of hedge kelp and ivy, or copsed old soldiers
who wouldn't lay down arms but made
a last stand on the hill and lean forever
on their brittle pikes, pared to the bone.

Every winter they stripped to bare branch
yet the eyes know this is no nakedness
to put on Spring anymore than the boxed dead;
sapless they're quick snapped by a passing wind.
The rooks caw off house hunting elsewhere
among the live leaves. Last year's tenement nests
perch like heads of drowned hair. They must learn
to build among oak and poplar, adapt
like the rest of us, raise the fledgelings
on folklore of how those skyships tossed
so that when the suckers deep in the hedgebottom
creep tentative, immune heads above blackthorn
dogwood, those ragged boomerangs their assigns
can wheel clamorous, gossiping home.

Song of the Stand-pipe

Look the trees are dying in the drought
beech and birch keel over
shallow roots clutch at crumbling earth
copper and silver become uncurrent
beaten too soon into autumn
yet the leaden plane
sheds again
its patched hide
with seventeenth century resilience
whatever civil war
the elements embark on
sun against rain
it stands
making its rough balls to propagate
citizen not recorded in the wild state
hybrid
tough cockney
that will uproot the paving stones
if we should ever
decamp
and lace its branches beautifully
over the crumpled streets.
When elm and oak
are bugged and broken
like love it will be here
nave and aisles
when the next first men
come wondering back
into the tumbled city
to begin again.

On a Drawing by Mervyn Peake

Pony on my wall, kiss dappled
widow-Peaked with cavalier mane
around you tumble leaves and sprigs
as if you pranced upstreet
processional or through fall lanes.
That tail is a fox brush for flirting
yet not to be masked and pawed
but alive and well on my wall. Foot up
bent knee and balletic hoof
in the first merrygoround
position, you go bravely towards winter
or whatever ritual heralds you
with strewn branches. Camp
rocking horse, circus, sloe-gin eyed
yours is a fantastic courage
delicate and strong as those hooves
that tread down nothing
your creator rightly left blank
which may be eternal snows
the white wastes of our minds uninformed
by your fourstep, the ground of our undoing
that we prance out of (there's no plod
of dear straining heavy horse can lift us
with his halt fringed heels. He teaches
other things.) If we're lucky
and will be carnivalled, flung buds
leaves, heralded into town, whirl
shrieking children in fright and delight
with our bravura of mane and tail.
Or, almost with a ghostly horn
you could be unicorn.

Antigone

*For Merlina Mercouri, Aspasia Papathanassiou
and the others*

Didn't you know Colonel Creon she had
as many heads as you this Antigone
was the fates that spun your life out; feet clad
in Hermes' new jet sandals she would cry
tragedies against you til you were glad
to tear off her poisoned robe; couldn't you see
the tyrant's lines propped on your schooldesk: Haemon dead
the pierced figure of Euridice

that should have told you then you couldn't win?
Some chose exile, walled up mute in foreign tongues.
One in a prison camp painted faces on stone
with fingers tipped in blood, icons of disorderly women.
Just in time you broke down her walls to save your sons;
now let the blind lead you away alone.

Sonnets For The Portuguese (1974)

The Astrolabe

Dead princes watch over you through my eyes
(who governed better or worse as their time
and temperament allowed) with ironic gaze
see you celebrate their sixty-year demise.

You must be princes now each one, learn
their craft better, seek out new spice lands
through our ocean of darkness. We too might turn
to follow you round capes we only half discern

as yet, through straits where delicate caravels
founder and all hands lost. Our twined spheres
could tell us where eclipses lie, zodiac scales
horizons; in this new trade no more blood rivals

as old navigators mapped each other charts
they swore by with fingers crossed and hearts.

Lisbon 1: Pedro and Ines

Your southern dawn comes late. 'I must go love.'
'Not yet; look Orion still hangs lusting
over Hesper Venus where she smiles above
the rooftops.' First trams cruise the dark singing
six o'clock prime in their wires; seagull or dove
over the blue-black hump of hill smears its grey wing.
Yawning workmen stumble from their hive
funnel down cobbled alleys to where the tides begin.

One fishing boat thrusts out a masthead light
while mouldered lovers murmur in my head
'Not yet.' 'I must.' Did they draw out their night
as we've sweetly sometimes done? 'Come back to bed.'
'My father watches us. I dread his second sight.'
'Dawn will come late enough when I am dead.'

Lisbon 2: Education for Freedom

The bookshops are full of paperback cookery
books with menus for three course democracy.
The brides trawl the streets arms round each other
boys and girls learning how this honeymoon paklava
is artificed out of bees' hard graft bound
together, earthly cereal reaped and ground
harvest labour no one skives out of except
the sick, the old, the sad and those who won't expect.

Old One-eye's buried at Belem though I
missed him in the cool crocheted cloister. He'd approve
your enterprise, invest a new epic in your future
burn through the midnight lines his other eye
award these boys and girls his Isle of Love
and ache to see your unworldly empire sure.

181

Alcobaca: Lovers' Tombs

Driving north through pine groves Isabel saint
planted to raise men-of-war, chuffing
behind lorries up your main artery
of economic health, we stop to eat
among trunks still tapped for resinous droppings.
About Alcobaca the trees bleed whitely.

Oh my lovers you lie across the aisle
waiting a resurrection that never comes
except in human hearts when you fly
out of stone shrouds into each other's warm arms
daily as the tourists con your bitter tale
guide booked in your grove of petrified trunks, hear you sigh
'Lie still my love, not yet.' 'The centuries unfurl
yet only they feed their lust.' 'Lie still my soul.'

Batalha

After the battle John One your bastard
married our Phillipa, Gaunt's fair daughter
if you can judge by Blanche her mother
Chaucer's duchess he hymned to line his hood.
Here in the globeround chapel they hold cold hands
golden sons about them but for me most that
boy we Englished early as our East gate
Henry navigator, plotter of new lands
gartered to gird the world while we sink
into a civil war of petalled white or red.
History repeats itself I was brought up to think
but we can't afford you those strides ahead.
Give us your hands again. Together we might
generate prodigies in faint heart's despite.

182

Coimbra

Two mating white butterflies are torn apart
by the car. Here they'll fix the valve; here
Ines was strangled; Camoens took his degree.
Where were you when your father tore out your heart?
Gone hunting? Oh yes you made them slobber with fear
her assassins, kiss her green hand, bend the knee
before you cut their throats but for learning, art
what did you do? In autumn heat the streets slumber
hot walls poster in red splashes a change of key.
At the brasserie tables over chocolate
students exchange fingertip kisses. 'Here
you will be safe. My father will surely see.'

'Who are those men at the door showing only their eyes?
If I kneel for this old king shall I ever rise?'

Braganza

Your Catherine dowered us with Bombay and Tangier
(history you will be the death of me)
but no bouncing child. Up in the old town
walled dogs and children and a stone bear
Celtic totem a later age made pillory
inhabit the dust with women in the black gown
of perpetual mourning, statutory wear
after thirty. She barren saved us a new
civil war, the arrogance of divine kings
forecast our path when her blood denied sons.

Legend says you were married here. I pray not.
That benediction lets a kiss of death
fall between you. May you have lived one heart
died one fused flesh no grave ceremony can bequeath.

The Border

We wind through mountains. The signpost
unwilling to let go would turn us back
through bleak serras where hawks ghost
haunting the scrub til I am every jack
quivering rodent. Behind us lie gilt wood
blue sketches on white tile, knotted stone
seakings and sculpt shellfish that artefact
your story where, Tagus straddled, rides Queen Lisbon.

Spill no more blood. Pombal built in reason
and geometry as well as stone, squares
avenues your lovers can take their ease in
live out their private and public affairs
with dignity. No-man's-land lies further on
between customs posts where you can't tell ours from theirs.

184

Nigerian Execution

They have fallen awry
the young men shot.
This one the bonds held up
this one they let drop
til his cheek rests on the earth
that one touches his toes
as they taught him at school.
Some were a plot
to pull down the state
others swept up
or simply confused.
Their licorice limbs bend
now before they take on
that rigidity their judges
have clamped to their minds.
I look down the photographed line
this one of course was loved
this lived alone with books
this child of Narcissus and Echo
grew drunk on his own voice
that was bloody
another a petty crook.
They will dignify their cause
but no one pulling strings
can jerk them upright anymore
though their ghosts creep into the town
to squat on the beaten floor.

Three thousand miles away
by satellite I mourn
the rest of their lives unborn
those islands of flesh and bone
mine
whatever they had done
sink on their anchor bonds
irrevocably
though the tides dash on.

Chilean Epitaphs

News, terrible news
cry us
terrible news.
Today a man cocked a machine gun between his teeth
and shot off
(they'll claim of course
he was made to
or murdered
as if it wasn't enough he should dynamite
our temple with the cheap
popgun of cops and robbers
or strafe our refugee column into the ditch
with his leaden logic).
Allende let no one deny you
the Colosseum of our round eyes
tracking the newsprint.
Your footfalls in our mortal dust
turn up thumbs
that can't redeem your failed and bloodless revolution.
Are we only to be dowried with liquid rubies?
Why can't fraternity come riding paper tigers
not these clawed carnivores
all vitriol spit and cagmag carrion flesh?
What were they afraid of
on your camera safari?

Death by retiarius is the most ignoble
netted like a cod til you choke
on dust.
But when the coarse fishermen let down their subtle meshes
for profit
no salmon heavenbent upstream
can avoid them.
You beat your head out on the stone quay
and the scales sicken and dull under the noon glare.

Now they are burning books in the streets
the coldsober soldiery. Neruda's
wound weeps him to death.

24 September 1973

186

Condemned: for 'Shelter'

Reading I am nine years old again
three in a bed, out there another four
our seven breaths hang in the chill fetid air.
Below the baby whimpers his lullaby of roachland
cradled above the livingroom's midnight uglybug ball.
Halfasleep I fondle my brother's pubescent prick
limp and pink as the raw runt
of a pound litter of sausages
a makeweight piglet I wish was mine.

We live by bread almost alone
with jam on it. Dinners bubble and squeak
their second or third time round.
The morning kettle is filled with eskimo splinters
that dewdrop the tap in the yard.
Hot yellow streams splash back from the rinked pan
while the draught under the door manacles
grimy ankles from across steppes of allotment.

So close it seems in the sour smell
from these pages, wounds scarred over by thirty years
bleed as at the approach of murderers.
Still I am childishly impotent to make
one least change in a life so like
the opening of mine. They are slaughtering
innocents with charity Christmas stockings
over their faces garnished with gold coins
of bitter chocolate and foil.

Like nightmares we can't pin them down
lash them to the wormy bedfoot, the crevassed
floorboards, spreadeagle them over the colander roof.
I hear Herod's soldiery in the street
calling for a young throat to whet
their razor edge. Heavy with her majority
Democracy stalks the slums, her liberty cap
shadowing a witch hat on the crumbling walls
for bedtime story. While reason nods
she too is mother to monsters.

Child on page 31, area drowned and barred
only Desperate Dan can get you out of there.
I came up by luck and love and all I can throw you
is this frayed rope of twisted words.

The Raising of the Morrigu

When they dredged her up from the bogside
with all the camera eyes waiting to see
there were holy men with their: 'Let us bray,'
but I answered them quick with my: 'No, not me.'

She's old and ugly as sin in a judgement
she sucks men's blood to feed her own
her bones are quicklime, her flesh is sulphur
she blights the land where a rose might have blown.

She's black as a crow, our northern vulture
she only knows one meaning to death
she rapes the young to her rank fourposter
and hugs them out of their living breath.

I'd rather go unarmed and nameless
I'd rather be a hero in bed
than kiss her skull and take her shilling
and be famous in the kingdom of the walking dead.

So sink her down with a concrete collar
don't let those children handle her eyes
they will prize them opals, rubies, pearls
and with every sparkle one of them dies.

Give me a woman whose body is comfort
whose warm blood honeys in a comb of flesh
we will hone our lust and sharpen our reason
and slice through her tangling mesh

to drop her back where the leeches spawn
where her bigmouth children suckle and play
with a stake through her ribs, a noose for a loveknot
til her legendary feet are nothing but clay.

The Ballad of the Blasphemy Trial

Oh there is a place in Parnassus
where all the world's myths stand
rank on rank awaiting
the sign from a poet's hand.

Some are long dust and forgotten
their papyrus mummy shroud
crumbled. They wait for a scholar
to call them out of the crowd.

But some have names of thunder
that echo the centuries through
Isis, Venus, Moloch
Thor and his hammer too.

Yet at the call of a poet
each must rise and come
and only one law is god here
they must be true to their name.

So up in the morning early
Lord Jesus came to the hill
and there again he laid him down
to do the poet's will.

For love is Jesus' forename
where he sits on Parnassus hill
and he came to do his best there
as any great myth will.

And when his task was over
he went back to take his place
and all the myths moved over
and smiled into his face.

Lord Jesus he was troubled
as he gazed at the world below.
He nudged Socrates beside him
and asked was it true or no.

He saw a court and dock there
he knew them well of old
he saw what was put on trial
and the vision made him cold.

'Oh I have stood in a courtroom
and now what's this I see?
They are trying a man at the bar
and all in the name of me.

Oh I have hung between two thieves
so all my stories say
and shall the law that broke my limbs
be invoked for me today?'

Then Jesus stood on Parnassus side
and tore his long dark hair
but Socrates restrained him
and spelled it out with care.

'Although we must always follow
and be true to our stories' truth
no such constraints can bind them.'
Lord Jesus gnashed his teeth.

'They have made me into a mockery
with their blasphemy of trial.
They have taken love, my given name
and broken it on a wheel.

I shall curse them in their blindness
I curse them in their pride.
They align themselves with Judas
and Pilate takes their side.'

Then Socrates gave him hemlock
as they sat on Parnassus hill
to soothe his deep affliction.
'Oh do not take it ill.

We both died condemned felons
though you by another's hand
and we must forgive our children
who do not understand.

Some in the name of reason
do things I shudder for
others for love invoke you
and stand you at their bar.'

But Jesus answered him fiercely
'Reason is not my name.
You must do as you have answer
I will not play their game.

I will go down to the courtyard
and hang me on a cross
while the judge pronounces sentence
and they will see their loss.'

Socrates looked down sadly
and reached below with his hand
to pluck the dear Lord Jesus
out of his own grandstand.

'Come up, come up, dear Jesus
they must not see you there
they will only think you demonstrate
and drag you off by your hair.

Remember your name is love, lord
come up along with me.
In time myths of love and reason
may cause the blind to see.'

Concordat

All sad white elephants ditching
their rusty tinribs under waves of weeds
gone home to die in neglected outfields
(that childhood fool hero
The Whispering Giant Who Didn't Want To Fly)
apotheosize in this shape
that flaps no rigid birdwings
but fishtails through thin air
porpoise limned and herringscale sheened
inherits Watt's kettle, Great Eastern
Stevenson's flung fantasy of lines
and bridges. Hallstatt knick-knock-knack
of warrior wheels, is for all our impotence
a shining ejaculation in the underbelly of cloud
is the firespitting defender
victory-rolling home to the heady Lethe of
downed drowning pints, lifts its
wise insect snout from the screen
with no disney cosy image but
sleek sheer shining is
the most beautiful Thing
We have never seen.

Kindred and Affinity

I have to say now
that I have shot and eaten you
in imagination and fact
these nearly forty years.

I have to say now
that filled with the sweet
savour of your flesh my mouth
runs with the juices of desire.

I have to say that
I can participate in the gun
raised snoutily at the sky
with a bead on you

or the wild chase that
hounds you into the earth
as my throat sics on my own
betraying bloodlusty bitch.

I have to say that
only my intellect and my
power for being you are
on your side, that I am

so much you I would fight
and master you Tarzan
or Adam if I could
or turn on the bank and rend

beside you the men, hounds
horses. I would say that if
you are hungry you may have
my dead flesh when I have

no further use for it
but if you should start towards hers
and I am near I would rouse myself
enough from my dying

to drive you like lemmings
over the world's end.

Song of Ignorance

Ding dong bell
Pussy's gone to hell
brought in a plastic bag
as though already dead
one fifteen you pay
to have her put away.
Who put her in?
The landlord rich and grim.
You can't keep a pet
take it to the vet.
Cruel to be kind
you won't leave her behind.
Can't just let her roam
I tried to find a home.
At least he doesn't cry
a hypocrite's goodbye.

Ding dong bell
hell's a basket cell
waiting for the gas
to make your terror pass.
Moggy black and white
howling in your fright
we are not so brave
I too dread the grave
when my spark like yours
flickers and expires.
Vivid in the sun
your days used to run
dodged the flying wheels
and the winter chills
now your nine threads snap
no escape from that.
Though your one life too
is unique to you
you must cease to be
when we turn the key.
Imagination fails
for animals with tails.
The species we preserve
but not the single dove

poison gulls as pests
so terns can have their nests
and thousands die
to titillate our eye.

Who'll pull her out?
The vet in white coat.
O shade of William Blake
for this tamed tyger's sake
you ring the bell
for Pussy gone to hell.
Ding dong bell
deep and dark the well.

Bestialry

Lemonchic

Laika forgotten
little bitch star
sometimes in the night
it worries me that
I can't remember
whether you are still there
orbiting among the other debris
a perpetual epitaph
pinpricked out of black tissue
skypaper of our
impatience and pride
that couldn't wait
but sent you tracking down
eternity
warped to your coffin
as surely as kittens
bound in a drowning sack
or if answering the whistle
of a pressed button
you became shot star
homing into ash.

We played God with you
Zeused you like Ganymede
but not out of love.
Did you think you were being punished
Callisto perhaps, for those seconds
only when your nosing dreams
beguiled you from duty
beyond the school walls
flirting your rump like ordinary dogs
not put down for headlines?
At the time they said
you were trained for it
as if we could take
obedience for assent
silence for unsuffering.

I make your small bones
this constellation for all those
who can't say no.

'Both Heads Lapped Perfectly'

I am you brother
who share our body.
At one time
they would have
put us on sideshow
with the bearded lady
the mermaid
the hermaphrodite
nature's prodigies
except that they made us
double tongued
four eyed.

If they urge me
I will twitch our paw
or thump our tail
to show we are
still alive.
I was a good dog
jumped through hoops to please.
Don't snap at me
try to bite me off
we have only ourself
and I'm afraid
of what goes on
inside your head.

Pecking Order

No harm comes to these
full corn fed if they peck
aright the face
the red light or the little tinkling bell
toc toc for the lottery prize
the pin ball in the socket
or the clay pigeons
of the fruit machine
shot down for the jackpot.
Don't blame them; they do
only what we did
in Dachau.
Shot with fear
and hunger we elbowed
our fellow skeletons
away from the food pail
licked boots, performed.
Caged they will prove
whatever is asked of them.
We fowlers who limed them
with our own reward and punishment
shall flutter in each dawn
touch down on bullet's end
and die to the pattern
of their bribed behaviour
who might have trilled and cooed
in the free courtyard of our wooing dance.

Lag Goose

Tagged the bird
braked in full flight
fell out of the sky
a tumbled handsized cloud
of grey and white flake down
snow or bunched sheets in the windowed washer.
Old lag, ticket of leave
laggard in formation
the lead devil took it hindmost
out of the pinking dawn.

Now it lies on the scrubbed table
nature mort rigid with the controlled rage
of Oudry at still life
The furled orange webs
are toy parasols that will
open and shut to a pulled ligament.
About the leg handle is a small band
'If found return to . . .'

So you were caught before
goosey, goosey or is it gander?
Who can tell til the belly is slit?
Once ago you were lured down
by the disc jockeying cries
to the snare of our curiosity
that would follow you about your seasons
mark where you spring and fall
where you are laid and lay.
Transfixed by the mesh and the numbing
pellet then as now you grew limp
to our will. The tag records
you twice shot, a lively statistic
plotting your graph to where you
and the winged bullet would meet
at a point called why.

Were you afraid, wary ever after
that first fix? We don't understand
the terrors of your birdbrain
our own metaphor minifies for us.

But we have always used you
quilled our poems and greased our palms
made Christmas and pantomime of you
painted you skidding down two point aheel
on some plashet of our nostalgic
first grey light among rufty-tufty reeds.

Small cylinder
go tell the recording computer
our grey lag goose is dead.

Cursery Rhyme

Flopsy bunny
your limbs fall down dead,
why did you beat
the wall with your head?

Brer Rabbit lies low
says nothing to us now
the mixytar baby
is holding his paw.

Run rabbit, run
the war is inside
the bacterial timebombs
go off when you die.

Your carcase will smoulder
and spread its ash wide
so brothers and sisters
shall bob scuts and cry

Where are our aprons
check breeches and all?
Hero Peter Cottontail
come to our call.

I am coming with Thumper
they loved him in the film
surely they'll listen
as we stagger and squeal.

They say that we nibbled
five million away
we poached off a fortune
and now we must pay.

Farewell to old England
to the coneyless coast
where the only buck rarebit
is served up on toast.

O brothers in hutches
get loose when you can
make love like rabbits
but be heartless as man.

Accident

Ahead a bird gunned down by the car in front
that spirts away in a burst of pain and feathers
flutters to the roadside. Anytime it might be me
bucking the breath out of a soft body
with my metal hide.
I sic myself on to retrieve
knowing I should cure or kill.
Undistinguished, pied like cheap bathroom lino
one in a million it drags its maimed leg
from my reach behind the wire gate
sets a bead on me with painted still life
bright eye I can't put out
shuffles with beggarly speed into a crater
for cover from my murdering touch.

'Beware guard dogs. Keep out.'
The notice barks overhead.
I remind myself of the common fall of sparrows.
'If we're that way,' the phone voice says kindly,
'after a dog that's been knocked down . . .'

There is a hierarchy in suffering.
The child next door dies wept by a street
while hundreds let fall their dried bundles of limbs
unremarked; my pigeon drags its broken claw
across my chest as a thousand broilers
slit their throats for the Sunday roast.

Yet I can't nod it off. It was afraid
of me and fear I understand.
When I go back it's dead
the head fallen awry, the feathers
softened to down. The dogs will find it.
It has attained, of course, a peace
in its hunched nothingness
and someone has thoughtfully painted over
the sharp eye with a fold of lead.

I know in the block beyond
the surgeon is fitting his scalpel
into the flesh of a man, a child run down this morning

drains vicarious life from a slung bottle
that the splinter of pain that stabbed
these ounces of hollow bone and feather
in this corner of the grounds
where they are building the new ward
is not a breath in the tempest of terror.

But it was afraid and I couldn't explain.
It was dying my death while for a moment
I died a bird. No sophistry of profit
or the fitness to survive
no humanity can absolve me from that communion
of animal fear
nor one pain cancel out another
though it go to the morning dustcart
expendable as cheap torn lino.

Conservation

Renard the runnable snouts in the dust
at the back of Deodar Road.
Behind his eyes pink coats neon
where Putney bridge halloos across the river
with hunting klaxon of Friday night gone to earth.
Chicken and chips he suppers from the daily news
ham fat, waxy skate ribs, bacon rinds.

He was out the day the gas came calling
reaching its green fingers down to his vixen and cubs
watched from a hill the men from the ministry
with their spades counting the furred lumps.
'Old dog fox I reckon he wasn't at home.'

Nothing to keep him now in the country
he headed for town, became part of the urban drift.
For a time at Richmond he lived among mild deer
til the cracksmen came fitting a bullet
between the does-eyes with a fine sense of proportion.

Myopic the old lady took him in.
She had always wanted a dog.
On Saturdays he trots demure at her side
in collar and lead along the shopping high street;
evenings he spreads his red pelt
for a hearthrug. In the attic trunk
the motheaten tippet grins beadily.
The fable has come home.

When the wind rises he lifts his head.
He is waiting for the elephants already
on their way from Africa rounding the Cape like whales.

Their grey legs piston the waters
their trunks trumpet spume at the stars.
They are coming to pull down the guyropes
on the human circus and plunge the ringmaster
shrieking into the sea.

Aesop in Suburbia

Quick brown fox jumped
over the garden wall
to his lady leashed
their fondling pet
in her kennel
nuzzled, nibbled
left his fuckmarks
in her burnished flanks.

Now brown fox
no longer quick
you bring mice, small birds
to your tumbling cubs
drawn over the garden wall
on the leash of love.
They have bound you too.

High-Bred

Children should be told this story
in nursery rhyme or bedtime tale
how he wasn't content to be gander
looking at my lady in her chamber
or goosebarnacled to the duckpond
but upped a swan, the king's dish
singing and silver. He was of course
grandson to the one who laid the golden egg
cousin to her who made a princess laugh.
No doubt he got his way by clowning
and promises of gilt on the gingerbread
but she who could have swanned off anywhere
dipped her beak and let him make
their bedtime story a nursery rhyme.
Nobody knows how to name their sport
as it ducks and dabbles in the indifferent stream
raucous as a gosling yet cygnet with her grace.
Let us all be happy ever after.

Lettice, second named for a dry stone region
clear as your eyes where the brooks fall quick and pure
waters you can safely drink though still the mists come down
the way's not easy, give us this celebration day your
blessing that we haven't failed you who are
so true it hurts to come at you athwart
who have kept a live flame you lit and blew into fire
and with your children, books, have unswerving wrought and
                                        taught.

Honest as your day is long Lettice then
who have outrun, outdone, testament's lie
that would pin us to three-score years and ten
whose first cry broke in another century
accept our love and homage for this day.
You are so much of this time it must go your way.

Travelling

For Dulan and Paddy

Happy as sandboys plotting for golden Venice
with treasure maps, phrase book, paged jewels
of fresco, I see your bent heads banish
for a time the tides gnawing our roots, your profiles
black cutouts stamped on days Guardi shrouded
or Canaletto crisp, as you pirate
loot to bear home, images only clouded
by their fecundity, an embarrassment of plate
embossed with seagods, inlaid with Venus pearl.
Let antiphonies sound for you, be double choired
in harmony as when their republican earl
married the sea. Among palaces be attired
in water and light, rulers of five days together
and your reign happy as sandboys ever after.

For Roy Fuller on his poems in Thames 5

A pain earlier he caught
an old man smiling in his glass
like Hitomaro years before
he bound it up with verse

pinned back his shoulders
trimmed the whitening moustache
began to act his age or youth
threatened apoplexy for a laugh

that wasn't quite in fun
met at a party, confessed
to illness, not quite mortal
but feeling not his best.

Chipper, dapper, I admire
your form, knowing already
I must come to share its content
if my pulse keeps beating steady

Know I too grow more like
my elders though I wear
my best clothcap askew.
Your boater's tilted to a rakish air

your father might have hummed.
No matter. We all come
in fancy dress to dance
to Willie's old-dog-tincan drum

early or late. Women come sooner
with that seachange of blood and fears
that dulls the saltiest itch.
Still dreams are theirs

like yours of young arms
and Horatian tears for boys
they follow through stream and field
puff up their eyes.

Villon's old crone was vocal
on this theme of wasting flesh.
Some girl there may be
in chic cavalier dress

like Rochester's with a taste
for older men. Take her as muse.
I'd like to see you still foxtrotting
to the pavilion's rainy close.

'Young and Old' by R. S. Thomas

They tell me you minister
a parish of the dead
where the graves run down into the sea
and on sundays sermon dry bones
to a handful of the valley's dying
or proffer a sip from your chalice skull
whose blood congeals to inkblots
precise mirror images of your horror.

I picture the children taking out these poems
with curiosity, bright bits of phrases
welded to a cold steel frame
that barely hides its asymmetric purpose.
Only the dwarf in the dunce cap
on the corner stool, carrying his huge head
with its fifteen years on a five-year-old's
body claps his hands with recognition
at the signal gantry he has made out
of your chill scaffolding and bits of
stained sharp glass.

Here the country doesn't comfort
or the town divert; love is a word
writ in chalk on a school blackboard.
The only escape from 'the initial contagion'
is to ride the stones as they march into the sea
erect in the foursquare tumbril of cause and effect.

Yet how the dry bones sing
among these pages so that when I close them
I want to weld bone and steel too
in your suasive tone; my own voice
demanding to be heard strikes shrill.
I hang these shapes
blunt scissored paper cutouts
among the branches of your yew trees
like a prepaid telegram
to which no one can think of an answer.

On His Blackberries Gone Mouldy

For Seamus Heaney

You should have put them down to turn to wine
to yeast with sugar, bubble for a month
then strain and siphon off in casks
let them lie still while a twelvemonth turns
watching to see no wild yeasts bloom
their sweet to sour, no vinegar fly
lays bitter droppings in their bloody depths.

Come the next year you could have run them off
last August caught, the sun and dark spiced fruit
the bramble gift, gratuitous, casual as sudden love
have lit another year, mellowed next winter's frost
with native Falernian, in heady classical
tradition of friendship and fireside.
Instead you let the mildew have them.

Not your fault of course; what you were brought up to
since the fall of limbs from that Judas tree
a rigor mortis that cramps us still
in crucifixion postures to blight
even the innocent berries on the hill
as if our hands were leprous from playing
with ourselves in lieu of others. You let despair
dictate their decay. Fruits can rise up in wine
love in the linked flesh, transmute by a barm of lust
sugared with words and gestures, laid by
in absence to drink and drink again
in the warm bed of winter
lightening our darkness, a gentle lunacy
we sip and sip to keep us sane.

Lost vintage of blackberries you squandered
preach sermons for me. Time enough
for a shroud of mould when the sun goes down
in our eyes. These autumn hills
are clothed with bracken for beds, ripe with
heavy fall fruits I can grow drunk on; overnight
mushrooms mark where we lay. Behind nettles

and the slung silver of dewed webs hang
the reached treasures I crush into words
that may light equinox tapers in later eyes.

You have to have faith in fruits, top and tail
pick, turn over, add your fermenting heat to theirs
cosset the chemical change that will power
a rocket at the sun so that drawing the cork
long after connoisseurs may take
pleasure in this limbec, the bouquet
of mingled sweat, regather
the clove and cinnamon light of our hillside
where pleasure grow for the taking.

In Memoriam John Berryman et Al

Poets you go down into waters
with your pockets full of
brazen images that wouldn't answer your pleas.
No one comes knocking on the ivory tower
with their hands full of need and terrors
or on day trip from Porlock.
At night the sirens swim up to flirt
their lamé tails at your windows
when there's no one at home to tie you down.
They offer you their mouths that taste
of tears from long communion
in your drowned seacaves
where you dredge for rhymes
a chalice of shared blood to sip
or their white round hosting breasts.

Old seadogs know their tunes well
becalmed, adrift, their mirrorsmirking
features, neatcombed hair, their blessed isles
for those in saga who have almost forgotten
the shuttle longing to and fro
that weaves a venus tapestry
to hang their bed, the hands that send
it carrier back and forth patterning
the hot afternoon with moist twined limbs.

Stuff your ears with wax. Too soon
over the darkening waves the tailed amazons
tridented with their threepronged god
will bear you down, give you a dagger
runed with old guilts to stab your love
and sink you in their bitter trough.
I don't know why you tripped it
into the deeps with ripples
snapping at your heels, exercising a last freedom
a leashed, docile dog you took for a walk
throwing it a stick you had to dive to retrieve.
I stand on the shingle that razors
my bare feet selfishly glad she whistles me back
from the murmuring tunefull edge
where good poets stumble and drown.

214

Mulepraise Long After

I'd tell you now we lovers are awake
if you could know where your slime quickens into shoot
green with new Spring, though rinsed through twenty winters
it may rest by this at the cliff's foot
last liedown before the waves take it
for fishfood, laverbread, the bony
mouths snap and mumble on the flesh that made songs
for lovers.

Your bones remain and the words to clothe them
for us to make a reliquary permanent
as ink. Most scribblers don't come, busy with
strife and the grey fall of their own
perpetual dust, shedding of dead cells.
Litanies of unfashionable
hope resolve cracked in waxed ears whose music's
bone on bone.

And those asleep in each other's arms don't hear
only these midnight oilburners who glut their ache
on rhymes, assurances that nothing is lost but time
and he's a thief will steal all hearts, fence
break them down to equal elements.
Liquored in communion, cups
running over with amber tears they stagger
arm in arm

with your talking Bran'shead for company
and the characters from gravestones for runes to guide
them home to a chaste bed. You said we must all lie
heavy as clay but not to embrace
just take it. You said kingdom never
comes except in joined flesh; that worms
eat us, and leaves trees spilled, that sucked clouds
whose white heads

were moulded of rain sweated from oceans
where dabs play, that eat worms from your slime and are eaten
by lovers who pluck keepsake leaves, bays for each other
all building Jack's house of mud and dreams.

But I say, that time and rhymes are all we have
that, if she can't hear, the words wash
from the page in brine, your syllables hiss
rain on the sea

gulped by the thief you set yourself
to catch by the foot; only in the sun that broods
on the shoulder of her Saint Martin's summer where I
drunkard and begger bask am I
renewed. Hollow the vowels boom and echo
when she is away, the park's
deserted and your birthprayers, changeling by
thieving hours

leave a cradle full of monsters mishapen
from the pretty children you wove of promise
and your own gone boyhood. I took at her young snap
where I can put my mouth to hers only
by courtesy of dreams and rage against
death, yours, ours, turning the keepsake leaves
of your hiccuped golden mythologies
cradling love.

You built your memorial Portmeirion
baroque among the black fields of sermon prose
and dun Bethesda verse. The sea rollicks to your
cadences as you command its waves
back to your childhood, pawing the beach
at your charms, and the unloving
cap your wizardry with visions I can only
build in her eyes.

Ode on Rereading Keats

No sir I will not; see I
dignify or abuse you with my own age
as if the month we shared
fell too in the same year
calling you, bright boy, sir.
You come to me, darkling
masked in my childhood
with the long dried elder flowers of wreaths
verse epitaphs through these pent streets
and tell me follow into that country
of eglantine and blackthorn
but it is winter and in any case
all my musk roses are dedicate
you come a life too late.

Then I might have followed you
myself, wanting fame too and half in love
with your prints, my steps
tracked so precisely, nine and fourteen
as if we shared the same sock size
I might step into your shoes.
Easeful I leant upon my window sill
in the fading day and saw you
dopple ganging through the fields
under a green sky warping to purple
and thought I might run out
to become you going down with the sun
ghosts walk at twilight
with kindlier beckon than at night.

Now you start at me out of
the pages trailing my life and yours like cerecloth
gibe that my day with its sweets
is gone too, that my years betray
our common growing pain.
It's easy to die, remember.
If she would with her own soft hands
pour me oblivion I could
slip out with a kiss as if
I was just going to move Venus' car

but I hover on her threshold
on the end of my hope
that she will unleash my bounding
and whistle me into the sun.

Too late you come over the black fields
set in winter. I have forgot
betrayed nothing you taught me
about beauty and truth only that
at last wandering my years
like countries I have resolved
that examination question you put
to the ages: she being all truth
is beauty, being beauty is
all my truth. At night she
holds me by permission
of that fancy elf. Apart I
wade through blood, give goblins
guest room, ride nightmare widdershins.

I sip my vintage, seven year they say
matured still not as old as me.
Painstakingly I pass the milestone ages
when it's significant to die: young at thirtyfive
choosy at forty or straddling the century's turn
inelegant posture with the legs apart
and easily brought down, til I don't care.
If I had known her then when we walked
rehearsing our verses in beechen green
drawing our rebel bows at wands
I might have gone glad to an early grave.
Now let me limp on as long as we can
armour ourselves with love against swords
she quicken into fancy with my words.

Ask me no moe Thomas Carew, Gent.

Why Tom Carew
they say you were no better
than you could have been
minor poet harping on one theme
not loud enough to turn
the slings and arrows of outraged
criticism though their fine scholarly mesh
can't seive out her true name
from those aliases of the perpetual blow cold
blow hot love war: spiced, spied Celia
or yours anonymously 'my mistris'.
Perhaps she walked only in your head
her lines sketched from wishes
like the flower maiden Blodeuwedd
but you went always with impeccable beat
rhyming your way towards the right true
and which is stranded on her breast
between tide and time
that would seachange her silver bay
more beckoning than
newfound vinland
and your thrusting prow.

If you had put your faith
in dignifying the moment
of leaf vein and flower's trumpet
they might have had you
stride giant among their low hills
or if you tinkered your progress
through the bedlam of vision
and Denial-quaking-sounds
academic overtures might have blown for you
from their other side and you stumbled
at last into recognition.
But you didn't falter your pleasured tread
any more than those elegies cupid headed
my love and I have remarked in weeping churchyards
though gossip would have given you
repentance without absolution
and the examiners will never forgive

your moist lip and neat poised form
adamant in lust that queries
their dried blooms and guilt frames.

Since I no longer know East, West
the phoenix' nursery, alembic of the fading rose
nightingale's incongruous tonic solfa
except through her, you intone for me
a ceremony of my flesh
of my body's worship in your major minor key
that makes us, her, me, you
as good as we should be.

On the Discovery of some of John Donne's Papers

Of a sudden your papers stable stained
I pilgrim through, relicts of your neat hand
riding pillion behind you Westward
jealous gods left East under angel guard
entombed while you're away, your lovers both
body and soul: brought to bed each nine month
or hung crossed every twelve to wrench your heart.
What could she do against that careful art
those ghost's bones but die too. Then you could pray
the two in one to take your breath away.

Long dying after, mortified in stone
you hid those limbs she must have loved and known
trothed to groom death you'd never turned your back on
bridal shrouded. Doubly I mourn Jack in Doctor Donne.

For Benjamin Britten: A Baroque Elegy

Let all the choir of bright Cecilia come
her singing spheres be void and dumb
as she bends low. His dying breath today
seeps in diminish'd sevenths away
and there in the mind's Elysium
crowd his English peers: Dunstable, Dowland, Lawes
and Byrd who sang that with Tallis music died
in notes that his own weeping words belied
for, against nature's lesser laws
music's immortal. Though each fleshly instrument
unstrings yet still she breathes into new ears
her merciless song, the bitter descant
distill'd of lust and tears
until that final chaos come
and all the world falls dumb.

City pale let the Wandsworth cherubin
their winter ceremony of dirge begin
and all
your history of song recall
from when the stars in harmony carolled round
our planet, to the mad sound
of gunthroats chattering death
a soldier's murdered breath
anger and anguish, the full score
of war and the pity of war.
You were only one when the world went askew
yet the terror, the waste, these never left you.
You speak for us all this century: the mud
of those trenched fields still sullies our blood.
Owen's words, your notes
diestamped them into our hearts.

Purcell I see you standing on the shore
as far as mind's eye can go (I can no more
if other times could be yours would be mine)
you wait to take the line
and haul the swart boat in.
Best, sweetest you must make
room for him there for music's sake.

'They paid you well then?' 'Better than you
who rented the loft seats for a pound or two.
But tell me when you set the dream . . .'
The voices fade.

A door shuts.
I shall never set foot in that country
we made together in my head
where you put my words to rites
and hero Piers ploughed us a half-acre.
Your door closing
is two thirds down the corridor
that leads to the one at the dead end
I shall go through into my dark.
We are pipers on the shore
printing their wet arrows in sand til the tides
flush through the rank saltings
unless somewhere a boy or girl
picks out a new tune one-fingered.
They are your children.
Today frost crinkles the pools to stillness.
Under winter's hand the earth is holding its breath.
Come Cecilia, take back your son.

4 December 1976

Suicide

Twenty years ago we met
and you are the first of us
who were young together
to die.
Often I was angry with you
hated you even.
Now you have taken out
one of the stays that rib
my consciousness
making me still angry with you
at the end of this non-relationship
therefore punished
by your sad slack body.
Perhaps that was what you intended.

So I sit here at midnight
making four bad copies of these words
on my typewriter
as you would have done
and missing the keys
with a rage
that could be your own.

Only Fade

I am surrounded by the dying
a hazard of my age group
white hairs frost your jowl
tantivy among the hounding swathes
in full cry after time.
My father figure gropes
towards the door unable anymore
to grasp at home away draw
since they resolve to a pattern of noughts and crosses.
As for nought he knows it to the bone
and cross he took up years ago, lightly laughing a bit.
It's grown now monstrous as if it had forgotten
he served long since, gassed, shrapnelled
more than any two bits of wood should have laid on him.
He waits about the house for the whistle
to go over the top.
Selfishly I want him as in childhood dreams
to go bravely.
This is a hand for me in case he falls back.

*

That night before this I was there
and you too
we had jokes about beer
you winked iconoclast
when the breath wouldn't come
to put out the words.
I went away thinking
you might as so often come through.
Today the wind whistled and moaned in your chest
a song not in your barbershop descant
but swansong.
Teatime you spat blood
but drank a supper of invalid pap.
At stool suddenly your heart sagged
in its bed of rotted lungs
your head fell back.

You are not to be forgotten
and warped by the sentimentality of death.
What Socrates said outacids hemlock.
You shall not be made to bow
now you can't anymore
with one wry touch
set the world aright.
Be rigid in death as bone.
Up that straight alley
they still pull the best pint.

19 December 1975

Eostre Sunday

Today tastes of marzipan; not the real
rich pounded nut paté but substitute
soya, bottle almond flavoured bittersweet
savour of wartime mingled with wet
primrose petals and moss. We have gone
a picnic in the sprouting wood, showered
with threats of rain between the sunlight
an Easter rite of paste eggs, blossoms
and larks high under the clouds for a goddess
of dawning year not the hanging man.
My mother presided: made the mock sweets
we didn't need coupons for. I think it was
her celebration that she had lived
through another winter's bombardment
this was truce before she fought her summer campaign
winning back ceded territories of lung tissue
foul weather had encroached on her breath. Now
with a Spring life restored. I feel it still
bred into the mind's bone; ideas of larks
the picnic in the wantoning woods call cuckoo
out of the city trees. The goddess in her cart
is on her rounds, making shoots, catkins, ears
eventually out of her falling grains
and why should I deny her tribute
of remembered soymeal marzipan eggs?
Is this not wartime too, we under time's siege
our hours torpedoed, adrift, wracked
winter and why she must still take her way
each day's spring?

Genetics

The night before he left my father cracked
the brown armour of shrimps, nipped off
the whiskery head with the black bead eyes
and the hard fantail in a labour of love
that had become a ritual of goodbye.
We never saw him again. To my two months
it hardly mattered but she must have lain alone
or pushed me as I knew from her Grimm's tales
my folklore I took her through: 'Tell us
about when . . .' along deserted streets that led
to a shillingsworth of gas I made her
slam the oven door on with my two month wail.
My hands were like his she always said
and yet I see her hands ghost in their
gestures, plucking at my own flesh, hangnail
dry cheek, eyebrow fern as she herded crumbs
across the tablecloth with sheepdog brown fingers
or the breadknife. He could never put together
took apart with his hands that may be mine
but left the elemental cogwheels, bike chains
in primaeval chaos on the newspapered floor.
She fitted them into working order. My hands peel
a peach for you, furl back that soft skin
from the sweet globe I lust to sink
my teeth into. We both know the meaning
of peaches. Yet I can't tell whose fingers
peel so lovingly, his or hers, male or female
maker or destroyer. I splay my fingers.
The stories are thirty years dead and like all
retellers I warp, encrust, unmake.
The hands should know. Or have they learnt new gestures?
The fingers more spatulate, life and heart line
less broken than theirs? She never left
but made of the threaded chains of sputem
her lungs powered a lifeline I clung to.
Yet the eyes to see peaches, peel and present them
the hands that strip them down to naked flesh
flushed with eager juice the lips suck up
are those that ripped the scales from seafood
and gave her salt, waveborn, the small pink serpents
that caught in the sea anemone's embrace
are questing, taken in, father's fingers.

Christmas: all at Sea

Snow spume on the decking.
With icicle fangs
the ratlines gnaw my hands and feet
hauling to spy where the land
humps its white belly
out of carved jet curliques of sea and
sheet mica sky.
You asked me today where my cabin is
that my fantasies should mould me
the runaway with salt in my eyes
on my lips
crowsnesting here above the ebon swell
of streets blitzed to dark this swart Nowell
when the tinsel angel promises again
to the silly shepherds on Calamity Hill
presents for those who show goodwill.

We must dare to dream
though my cracked alto drags toward curtain
my breeches are too tight
Davy Jones hornpipes on the tilting planks
the bells weavil into our ears
toll hardtack
come down to the quay in your softest sleep
and lift a pharos handkerchief towards my craft.
I'll climb my mast of mindblown glass
while the cold flakes sperm around me.
Outside slate rain puddles our town
and anybody's child is stabled in
a battery highrise
Midnight: I sextant my course by Venus
the donkeys are taking the lifts
and miners wreath holly on their picks.

14/2/76

This palace
unlock it with key number 14
don't be afraid.
No Bluebeard terror dangles
from a ceiling meathook.
It will let you into a garden
not, like Alice, keep you out
looking down the kaleidoscope tunnel
to vistas you can't enter.
This garden is half formal
there's a clipped hedge
in shape of a heart
and below the terrace
a pond and fountains
who are lovessporting, venuses
squirting from breasts decorate
with moss and lichen in rococco pattern.
Enter the house: there we can see ourselves.
Do you mind that the mirrors
align you beside me with the benediction
of nearly a decade
that my lines sag or wrinkle
as time draws his scythe
through the silvered image
the false back you can't see through
making ripples in our clear stream
that make for an inevitable shore?

Love, step out of the glass towards me
and the birds take off
whirl about the ragged pre-Spring sky
to drop down pairing
so our true mythology renders.
Will you come down again in these old sky-trod tracks?
I am following; herding sheepdog or hawk
into another year's tu kuroo on the window sill.
Don't fly off too far.
As I grow old and fat I might miss you
and moult weeping on the barren ledges.

Fugit

After eight years our watches no longer keep time
I mean those time pieces we bought each other
mine elegant black to remind me
how Thanatos tossed his hearse plumes
yours heartshaped, rolled gold, my pitch
for a stake in your country
they falter together, race, fall silent.
The clock doctors coax and charge.

I know their sickness.
Long ago, yesterday, I said
bartering. 'Ten years.' Programmed they begin
to run down entering our ninth year.
Who could have known we would stand here
as if yesterday you came towards me
jewelled through pigeons
across a station where the tracks led everywhere.

Let us begin again
on two new watches.

Summer Fruits

You bought me apricot flesh
perhaps because we couldn't taste each other's.
I sink my teeth into it.
It's sweet like yours
but yielding to dissolution
You yield and yield but
there's always more to be going on with.
Always after I want to say
soon, soon again.
Apricots cloy.
Two or three or even half a dozen
and you have to say no more now
so that then I can't imagine
ever wanting them again.
But after a taste of you
my tongue reminded
of our short season
yearns for a glut of your sweet fruit
and what I can't devour
I make into this sour wine.

Chinese snow poem without illustration

Tell me sky
will you fall
obliterating the year's scrawled characters
mess of rooks' twig droppings
so my lady can run
onto your feathered page
and write
whatever she likes
with scooped up handfuls
footprints
scuffs
in her caligraphy of pleasure?

Now I should be able
to surround this
with falling flakes
tonguecold snowfruits
white fur capped mountains
but my fingers freeze with tiredness
and the ink gels from my incompetence.

Forgive me, snowqueen.
I am doing my best.
You melt the icicles
as these images try to sketch them.
The words run together
until they are one symbol
standing up like a snowman
with hotcoal eyes.

In Spring when the paths are open
we'll climb slowly, with the ice
cracking in the streams
and the sun licking the hillocks beside the path
smaller.
Tell me as we go up to the treeline
where we shall spend the night
in a lodging dangled between snow and stars
which do you really prefer:
snow when we make love under coverlets
or sun when the sheets
suck up our sweat?

233

Now it's winter
come close and let me keep you warm.
There are crystals in your hair.
I have made you another snowpoem
to calendar our love
and to charm your white wishes
out of the sky.

Long, thin banner poem

I can pen haikus
rime terze, chime sonnetts
but at the moment midnight
I unfurl
these long high cries of lust
as intoned by
Magdalenians under a canopy of bison
Egyptian mummies
libidinous vulnerable as a sparrow
Catullus
unDonne my master
and aching acres of graffiti
on hotflush lavatory walls.

Such skywriting's out of fashion.
When I was small
aeroplanes trailed
smoking messages
across the sky
madrigals of war
making headlines.
Love makes history
though the textbooks
call it abdication
as Antony trailed Cleopatra
and they're more concerned
with who downed whom
on the wasteground after school.

I prefer the pastime of adults
your smile and invitation
'Come into me'
breaking frontiers, formalities
without rhyme or reason
cadenced, free
'Come into me'.

The Spring wherein everything renews

Beyond the car windows late Spring puckers the grass
unhedged oceans for a strayed March wind to gust in
where no butterfly tacks, no rabbit bums a white scut.
After days hung limp as November washing
on the backyard line that sags across my childscape
soggy with old tears a near half century
should have wiped, the hedges motorwayside
are snowed again with May and we time's creatures
stretch out of wintersleep. Street caverned

snugged by central heating, draught excluded
still our blood flows thin as Capricorn sun
congeals as the garage thermometer drops.

Wicked late Spring flickers past
the copper beeches fresh as new blood
promise of summer in plumping lambs
the blade will pare down
as if we needed still
the splashed stone of midsummer
to make our sun rise. The buttocks
of cyclists hoe a bright furrow
between car and field.
They gather at the icecream van
their bikes pitchforked anyway
their sweatshirts sickle dark at the armpits
and with legends that separate them
into a masonry that knows where it's heading.

It's better to be like us I think
going nowhere except home which is
where we are as the old wives used to say
sudded up to the elbows or turning a slow mangle.
Such phrases are out of this time.
I dress them again as midsummer comes round
my offering on the common stone
that needs only heart's blood to bring in tomorrow
while our Spring climbs bubbling into the sky
in the small, mottled body of a lark.

236

We have to remember in our city cave
that outside the fresh season new flushes hot green.
Yet we have to remember that though leaves break
from stripped branch every year nothing changes
though the fox comes out of its hole
to wipe its face in the sun
the lone yellow butterfly curtsies in the sunlight.

They do what they can and when.
They will invade the cabbage patch
overturn the dustbin, aren't bound
by ought only must. We can make
a desolation outside the car window
or Eden of the intolerable loved world
out of a little heap of golden butterfly dust
and the potholing city
and make it again each for other
as you make it for me now with a hand
on my thigh afloat on the rippled grass waters
of late Spring.

Taking Down the Runners

Last night the first frost. Time to take down
the twined hop poles of runners, a scene
more favoured of painters than poets.
Backs bend, arms stretch in the labourer's
seasonal gymnastics. Overhead
a jet scores across a pane of frozen sky
on its daily migration. The watering pail's
topped with a glazed lid fallen in the night.
I heft a tendrilled stave. In the middleground
a rout of children riots in shipwreck
through the adventure playground. I shuck off
the stiff green curls, with here and there a hasbeen
that missed the pot like a broken ornament
discarded with the Christmas fir, aware
I am making ritual
out of an annual job.

The birds have flown except those stayathomes
crumbcadgers our natives on a dole
we mete out in return for trapeze tricks.
The strawberries still greenfruit foolishly
or lay a snowflower on the chill bed of earth
with foretaste of mayblossom. Old habits
die hard. I am easing again promise
out of petals, a dream of white flesh
sovereign against decay out of flowerheads
the next frost pounds to mush. Only in
the mind's eye can buds bloom through winter
against the misanthropy of nature
that would cut us all down to size. I mash
the green garlands for compost and stack the poles.
Remember the vert cascades
of their August beanfeast.

My breath hangs like a horse's in the air
or steam from a rich dropping that would feed
the strawberries or next year's tall vines.
My own skin reeks as I cuff of frost and earth.
I turn indoors with my load of compost thoughts
culled from cold leaves and commonplace

as pulses. What we get from nature's round
is comfort in the Spring's return, renewal
though not we walk again under buds.
Yet as I thaw my fingers they speak in pangs
their individual blood, much more this body
the earth will break to humus yearns after
painful life, knows itself now twined, curled crisp
upon its hard pole spine death will unstack
tumble its vertebrae
to nourishing bonemeal.

Oh my dear give me your warm flesh til that last
frost fall we can't, soft or sharp winged, migrant fly.

Angel and lady: not Pontormo's painted
pair kept apart to a Keatsian never
in fresco their limbs and robes untainted
by age and lust's still circling weather
but their ghost-faces, our postcard couple
I'm pandar to, bringing their pared flesh together
here on the bookcase bed for my subtle
secondhand voyeur's impersonating pleasure.

Grey tips his pinions' gold nourished on mortal air
honey heavy he swopped for heaven's thin atmosphere.
A crazed line says she's seven years older
I join their paled blue lips that must show colder.
He has no lily, no generating dove
they'll bear no holy children but their love.

Like revolution you have to be made
over and over again; otherwise is atrophy
a slack and creeping death, a corpse smell sprayed
with scent to keep the sun's tongues and the flies away.

You have to be every morning a collect
for chasing the dark and nightmare's hoofbeats
that pound home loss and fear, demons erect
with whip and spur through sleep's trench by trench retreat.

You have to be reborn every deadly September
from its harvest of wept leaves our North cries down
til the rough rain outside our windows falls tender
through the tropic of our bedded afternoon

as I make her over and over: promises
of renewal in our joined and living flesh.

Sunstroke

Heat brings the summer boys out of their shirts
barechested they vaunt their toasted muscles
in the park, cast-off vests like banners at the trail.

I drive you through them wondering
if this one or that beckons with a twitch
of browned shoulder, uneasy til indoors
you take all your clothes off
and not because of that sun.

THE GARLAND

Carmine Veneriana

Carmen 1
On Strozzi's Mars and Venus

Lucky bloke she's got you down there
while the imp pulls off your boots.
That's a something to remember
when you're twined by daisy roots.

Predatory Venus grips you
shoves her tongue into your mouth.
That's the stuff to get you going
like a rainfall after drouth.

Spiritual lovers tell us
how the clouds their souls enmesh
but there's nothing late news final
as the dark night of the flesh.

Come then Venus lay me back there
hang your heavy breasts above.
I am growing nightly older
give me one last taste of love.

Carmen 2
Song for an Irish Wolfhound

I am Venus' lucky lapdog
I pick up her gloves and shoes.
Tell me, tell me, passing stranger
whose lapdog are youse?

Tell me if you howl and whimper
in the kennel cold at night
or if sometimes, lucky dog
you are called to see her right

lay your head between her soft thighs
lap and lap until she comes
or are chained like me at evening
in this kennel of heart's slums

where the moon looks drained and pasty
never lights a lover's heart
and its beams can scarcely pick out
any passing tart.

Yap and yap as Venus' lapdog
who will take your part?

Carmen 3
Whore and Piece

When you come back home from battle
and you drop your spear and shield
leaving just the simple swordblade
in its sheath barely concealed

lightly into bed you leap then
wrap your arms around the prize
suddenly she turns her back
and begins to close her eyes.

What's to do then hero-conqueror
force your way into her charms
or be tender, smile and hold her
sleeping in your conquered arms?

I am not the one to tell you
night by night I weep and pray
that the dawning near tomorrow
sends me a victorious day.

Carmen 4
Skullsong

Heine's racked there in his attic
like the princess with the pea
half a dozen mattresses
can't disguise the pulse of pain.

Great venereal bitch you screwed him
up and cracked his balls and spine
still he wails above the streets of Paris
stanzas of the one he never had.

Cockney Keats a-dying youngly
he too felt your loss and pain.
'I should have lived and had her,'
that's the beat of his last line.

Come then poets late or early
Venus holds you at your death
her last will is what you utter
with your dying breath.

Carmen 5
In Memoriam

Only for you lover she has no compassion.
Small birds can have her palm to peck
but her hands are tightly folded
when you want her to pull down your zip.

Yet she can walk with long gone lovers
through the landskip of her heart
where leaves fall, hands lock, buns are buttered
and memory holds the toasting fork.

Carmen 6
Venetian Glass

Should I die my hair
like Aschenbach
face powder?
Kind friends say so.
Venus says 'No.
These are my accolades
got in my service
emblems of mortality.
Wear them for me.'

Carmen 7
Venus and the Handmaid

Venus what is this you bring
a handmaid on a leading string?

And what is this that I'm to do
pleasure her and still love you?

Better to remain still true
pleasure death and yet love you?

Carmen 8
All Clear

O harsh siren
I am bound down
but my ears are unstopped.
Twenty years have left me
late doldrum forties
and how can she still
welcome me home?

In her hall I shake my grey locks
expecting her to start back
except that the silver spears
prick among her hair
arguing my cause.

Yet still the suitors
thrust a leg, clutter the benches
empty the cellar, lay siege
until with my eyes
I shoot them down
leaving two middle-aged lovers
going hand in hand
towards bed
where silver may be still
prime ore.

Carmen 9
Firelight

Venus you say you are old now
you want to say adieu to love
and sit with your glass by the fire
skirt spread to warm your thighs.

But you brought me up in your worship
though I'm old and ridiculous too
to be panting after your favours
what else am I to do

imprinted with love of you through
down to mind's marrow and heart's
if it has any hand in this business
and isn't just a muscle of sorts?

Better to be old and a fool
than pretend it wasn't worth the game
of lighting a votary candle
when you know you're still scorched by her flame.

Better to be daft and obscene
than be ashamed of that once-has-been.
Venus though the night strikes chill
I burn still.

The Garland

1

Over my long wound now she lays her mouth.
Her mouth on mine sucks out the stinging hurt
poisons, deep inflamed sores that ate the veins away
and let the blood seep through. Her hand on my face
wipes the stains of time and grief. As war wounded do
I selfish take caressing oil and wine
to suture this weeping cicatrice of mine.

2

Dame Doulce Mercy
be kind as you are named
Denial, Shame and Fear
drive beyond your land

all that fair country
where I would lay my hand.
Let dear Pitié
bring me to that strand.

Dame Doulce Mercy
give your lips to mine.
The giant Chastity
has left me here to pine.

I sicken now and die
within his ghostly power.
Dame Doulce Mercy
give me your healing flower.

3

I am aware that I hold in my hand
a bird I had no right to call down
that its heart may stop
and its fine bones snap
in my clumsy grasp
but bloody as all hunters
while its soft breast
beats against mine
and its wings are still
I cannot let it go.

4

Names come late now heavy with accretions.
Behind yours stands a small boy
snottynosed and not very bright
a tubercular librarian, gaunt boned
a night club madam, a duchess
Lawrence might have painted. Your daughter
is named by chance for my mother.

Yet we remain two people meeting
for almost the first time
with no history except what we care to write.
Still I wonder what ghosts line up for you
behind my unloved, art deco pseudonym
of a movie queen whose charms always left me cold.

5

Faint fragrance hung about me all today.
I place in it as young girls used to lay
white hopes in perfumed trunks against their wedding day
my trust that you'll not turn away.

6

That you were sick with your first child
and so can't unqueasily hear
certain old songs even now
though a year later when he was beprammed
all your tunes were for singing
I add to my first conscious picture of you
in duet your cheek against your daughter's
that made a music in my blood
I dare ask you dance with me to.

7

Unnightlit now first time since childhood
she sleeps secure: the only tread
on the stair of her dreams her lover
come across the dark to drive fear afar
with armsfull of flowers.

8

This child's no manger where to rest its head
a brat the parish certain won't admit
begot in lust as all such bastards are
and yet a little love for all of that.

I've left it puling on your doorstep here
knowing your heart will have to take it up.
I'll pay for nursing and your tender care
in kissing kind to fill your loving cup

and when I see it hang about your knee
I'll say the cheeky runt takes after me.

9

It's always told from her side of course
the dazzle of the turning wheel
the spot of rose bright blood
a hundred years of dreams.
But what about him?
What about all that hunting
up early and out in mist and dew
following the prints of frail deer
through the changing seasons
so that when she woke and said
looking at him out of does' eyes
'You've been a long time coming, my prince'
he fell on his knees and wept.

10

Not enough effort in French I see
and a failure to keep bedroom rules.
Were you in training already to fulfil
my fantasy of the French maid in the cupboard?
Your English grammer advanced rapidly
under a new mistress
and at dancing you showed neat footwork.
Games were spasmodic.
It seems a new school
brought out the best and worst.
If that ten-year-old
whose world had undergone a red shift
wept at night I hold her now
in my arms against that childish pain
though I see that in painting
you had little patience
with anything at all difficult
and wonder how I shall make out
who am a portrait subject
for your eyes to make fair copies of
crevassed, demanding as any banker
Lawrence painted for brass.
But your free compositions were delightful
and your style original and vivacious
as indeed for your engravings on me now
I must report the same.

11

Rehearsing love because we can't make it
I chart my way towards you
and plot those soundings
you can't believe I took.
Is it not what you wanted
to be loved?
Would you rather like Echo
pine unheard in the woods?
What shall I do if my big bones
the solidity of my fleshly self
affright you
if beauty didn't really
in her heart of hearts
want this beast?

12

For all my faults correct me now
while they're still young and pliant to your love.
Mothers are kind that teach their children so
their wild rude ways don't monstrous grow.
You'd do as much for any seedling bed.
Weeded your roses make a finer show.
Be brave with secateurs, deadhead
my ranker vices: cut them down to size
or root out quite that in your eyes
nothing in me but fair prospects rise.

13

I would have you know me through and through.
Here's me and here: aged three in a stolen
sandpool I'd driven the boys who'd made it from
sockless with a stepbrother, perfect
prefect·in a ranked school shot
another woman's lover, drunk with a dark pint.
I lay them all at your feet.

Now give me yours. Girl, wife and mother
yet in none do I see true that look
that turns to me and none could deliver
your body's warm sculpt ivory
or those eyes love rings deep seachanges through.
You were holding yourself wary against
the camera's probe. Now you let my loving gaze
enter to make brandy snaps in my head
I'm proud if your closed shutter always before boxed out.

14

Do not my girl warp as a window on love
twoway distorting mirrors out of the past
that you weren't first in my heart
or I in your body, lace long welts
over its tender young skin, make
my old words a spell to sour
between your lips and mine
this promise of kisses.

Let love's alchemy mint new
in each other's arms, old hurts fall back
as we retrace the way to that gate
bitter sword sheathed, sinuous guilt snake
trod down, into the garden
I hold steady in the true glasses of your eyes.

15

It's easy to be brave in your arms
to boast, 'When the pain comes I can bear it.'
Yesterday your mouth on me so I said
having no mindsight then of how the blood
starts from the gash between us, fool's words
illusory as the sulphur veins
in the black diamante of seamed coal
that crumble in the fire's grasp as this
cold flame of absence shivers my flesh.
I should have known. Once you turned off
down a sliproad misnamed, brutal
as any city cut and I raged
at my slow death. Two lovers joined
in my carriage can make me weep. Why not we too
sit there, my lips touch your cheek?
So how am I surprised by loss and grief?
Oh credulous as rich men with all their stock
about them I laid up no gold store
against this bankruptcy, painted none
but brave dawns cossetted in your arms.

16

It's like breathing this love: it comes
so easy to me. It breaks into smiles
laughter at shared childish jokes
or sight of you coming downstairs
or last always through the barrier
afraid I won't be there
a childhood fear I inherit
from that portmanteau you bring with you
and open for me to show the dress
puffsleeved with a cherry on the pocket
you were bought postwar holidaying
on roller skates through another country
a Victorian child strayed
into movieland where the rules were drawn back.
I try to pull them aside now
to show our sea prospect but my need
makes me clumsy. I want you
rollercoastering hand in mine
down this freeway where we only have to
catch our breath to kiss and never stumble.

17

Did I sing you to me with my dark need
as I remember some black bloke did
in a picture whose name I've lost in time
making alone by his bush fire night music
that reached a handful of notes out to
the girl he fancied, brought up missionary
schooled to piano, so that she couldn't
help but come though you might have thought
if you hadn't seen the frame before
it was her trolling of the darkie bush
after sunset that led him on while he'd been
paying out long twinings of limed chords
that wrapped around her wrist, waist, ankle
and draw her to him. So which of us love
was it? You coming after or me calling
and now does it matter except in chronicling
that dream history we tell and retell
as I call and recall to keep you coming to me?

18

Map flat I trace the way you go
through a land in springburst
that has always before hurt you
with its first that can't last

its blossomy marryings
that shake down so soon
themselves their own confetti.
Autumn brings my gloom

when those branches you drive under
will hang with windfall fruit
drop-heavy. Now love it helps
to straw your West wandering route

with these petals or those remembered
bridemaids who saw me kiss
you under their flounces
of ranked pink and white marriage dress.

But how can I here sit petticoated
by their shade and not dream and dream of this?

19   *Evening Call*

As we speak I can hear too a blackbird
letting its heart out over fields dark after rain
from the chestnut, white tapers snuffed by summer
overseeing your bedroom window.
Across forty miles his voice descants yours
beating his bounds, tells the twilight
he is nested, his kingdom marked
by sung staves you mustn't pass
as children map lines on air
or in chalk, slight barriers of wishes
a heedless foot falls through
shattering sandcastles. A nesting hand
can snap his fence of sound
strew his walls in wisps, hard ground
fledgeling or egg. Marauders starve him
from his halfacre where he gods it
til Spring and summer lie at the chestnut's foot
perished. Same sort of singing fool
I too cast these frail guardian threads
about where my heart has lighted.

                                                        June 1980

20

Wakeful I keep a distant watch over your dreams
as I've seen leaves silhouette against aging night
heard birds begin while you breathed quiet beside me.
Last dawn you dreamed falling and woke asweat.
This hoar morning I hold you from nightmare hooves
though you can't feel my warding arms. Oh when you start
and cry I would be nurse and lover come to say
no white Alp but I will melt its snows with kissing.

Vaterlo

We are waiting at the barrier the lovers
I can pick out at least two more. I tell myself
you will be at the end and last through
your shoes coming off the length of the platform.
You will look so beautiful I shall wonder
what lucky bastard you're meeting. Looking out
I miss the other's greeting and you too.
Suddenly, puckish you're there
and I'm disarrayed, unable to kiss you
as I want. We talk of late trains
while my eyes brim and swim with Irish easy tears.
The others have gone off arm in arm
or stiffly not attune. They named this station
after our best battle not caring
about the meetings and farewells
its iron roof would house, the dyings
resurrections it would preside over.
It's right we should meet here: you as daughter
of the regiment, me might have made corporal.
What a fuss there would have been
unless they'd seen me as Europe's conqueror
in a British warm, if I'd eyed you
on church parade. He wanted the world.
I'd settle for a trooping princess
looking down from her high horse
as now I'm looking out. From up there
the hill falls flat. Only from below
you see the contours clear, the lines
we drew with compass point in plasticine
to plot steep scarp or gentle slope
on wet afternoons smelling of geography
worlds apart. How dare I now ask you
to chart our new territory, toil up
from ridge to ridge? Yet I'm here again
your train pulling in and the lovers waiting
and I turn with a touch of the old soldier
to where shoes falling off you walk the platform plain
towards me and our soft truce in each other's arms.

Tree House

From that window you looked down at dark yew trees
yet you can hardly have reached the sill unless
it was benched and cushioned where a child's knees
could be drawn up under her utility dress
for a good read and the occasional glance
down into the grounds below. Sepulchral
those branches weren't for you. Happy chance
had set you down where you were loved though you tell
me a story of childish shame that makes
me bleed. Yeats etched this path true lovers go
to tread each other's infant stumbling steps
put on the uniform of childhood. Just so
I do, glad that for you the year was a straight beech tree
while autumn bent the bitter yew for me.

School Stories

Here you were eight. I kneel with your sharp knees
digging into the hassock, leap the beech
ramparts on greenstick legs that dragged the waste
of the road walk to send 'Dear Mummy' pleas
for a mouthorgan and pony tales that teach
my heart new curvetting circus tricks in haste
while it still, old dog, can learn. At the gate
swung the gardener's kids who couldn't read or write.

I read today that eighty per cent of London
seven yearolds don't know peas grow in pods
nine out of ten in our land are urban
schooled: pavement and highrise their walks and woods.
This you know too and tune your listening heart
to where I linger with them swinging on your gate.

Country Church

Under your name I put mine to show we were here
coupled in the visitor's book forever
the nearest we may get to a register
but for those who come lovingly after, quite clear.

Mulberries

So tender to the touch they should shake down
quicker than I can pick them but they don't.
Each bruised nipple has to be fingered
before it will give itself, almost hardens
under my hand. In the tree teepee woven
of shapes children cut out of green paper
as very leaf, stalked tight to their twigs
the fruits hang, Christmas ornaments strung
inside out. Pirates must pierce or run
the foliage foil to spoil them. I crouch
in the webbed tent where undersea light strains
through the live fabric while a blur winged wasp
tacks from fallen sweetness to sweetness
honeying. I let him go and stretch
on tiptoe for the darkest drops that may
bloody my palm or wine me when winter comes.
It seems all my life has been a reaching up.
Now in this autumn in your garden love
falls about me prodigal as shook down fruit.

'I love you'

Nothing is until it has been said
words speak louder than deeds
because I grew up in a world
where endearments weren't part of life's needs.

Until over thirty no one called me
darling; conductresses
went as far as 'love' or 'dear'.
We were locked out of caresses.

actions were ambiguous tongues
that might mean just duty
compliance or habit. So I nag
with my love token's banality

proferred by every popsong, lover
mute except for this phrase
I repeat til you must be sick of it
who had too many words outpoured, were raised

on verbal excess and perhaps can't redeem it
yet I beg you accept that cross my heart I mean it.

Suburban Station

Bid to look out at the level crossing
to check if Bowers are still there for buns
I note the late twenties black and white shopping
parade set athwart the way the train runs.

Those are the stunted pines, that's the golfcourse.
If the window could open there would be
blended with sweetpea scents from ranked gold gorse
a faint bathtime tang of the near sea.

I can tell you who hate change it must look
much the same, skin deep at least, glimpsed as you said.
I can almost see the shop door jerk.
The carriage smells suddenly of new bread.

Something snaps in my heart at the knowledge
I can never print you memories black
on white as these, only late-comer wedge
a foot in your door and hand them gift-wrapped back.

Winter Still

Winter stitched us in early this year
combed flock over hedge and field
Laid a chill chaste sheet between me here
you there, til my blood's congealed

runs sluggish as any icebound stream.
Look down through the glassy wall
that tombs me in. Stilled waters dream
unmoved by fishtail; no call

of wildfowl wakes them; the weeds stand stiff
in their glazed shrouds, frost agate.
December's here, old face of grief.
Its ice splinter's in my heart.

So my world waits clothed in this little death
until you come to thaw it with your breath.

Semi-skilled Lover

Nothing like her ever came his way before
so he is a bit off his head. He welds
'I love you' under the bonnet of her car.
It is a passion so sharp it almost gelds

him. She doesn't know whether to laugh or cry.
Her children mock his boots wiped on her door mat.
Everything she has now fits, goes. His try
is to smooth her path, have all her needs off pat.

Yet he can never come at her, must fear to be
always the eager mongrel tolerated for
its willingness to please. Lopsided he
may clown to ingratiate, not be shown the door

dreading always the shadow over her threshold
of some smart talking *Times* turner, A or B.

The Millgirl's Burying
for Gracie Fields

With you out goes that running tide
we paddled in, skirts hefted high
and shrieks when waves wetted our trouserlegs
gartering our skimmed milk calves
those little dangers an icecream cornet's cold
and a couple of pints would soon put down.
We were so brave then in our fear
but your wave and bandstand carried us along
to the pier's end. What the butler foresaw
couldn't frighten only titillate and soothe.

You were woven of primal goddess stuff.
You found an island as we've always dreamed
thumbing the brochures for our package tours
where you were dame of sun and wine
and Roman emperors had drunk and dunked
their gross unfavourites in the salty wash.
You healed all that as you had benisoned
the mill, co-op, mote-spored aspidistra
and a warped tongue (by genteel standards)
into stardust that could have clogged
your frontroom piano keys, but didn't.

Your geographical shift
sounds as you used to lift
into impossibly true falsetto
the note to tell us
all keys can open
and you even showed us
some of the doors.

Old Long Sin 1980

Worth is it to scrawl on a darkened shore
when you can't halt the tide that drains the words away
and January winds whip through mind's flesh
to pare the wil' down to unyielding bone?
When we were kids you sewed in against winter cold
chills blained raw through spuds in undarnable socks
thin overcoats let Boreas blast his shotgun through
cold candles under our noses were cuffed out.
We shuddered then with frost not rage and fear
as I do at gnarled hands feeding
the last coin to the meter's grinning slit
at old skin hyperthermically sealed
against the draughts forever. Where's care?
Doled out, pittanced while New Year bells toll in
the bad old days again. I scribble this
graffito though the tide washes it out.

For The Freethinker *Centenary*

Thought is never free. It is bought in pain,
loneliness. Comfort clothes conformity.
Thought's a dole child, threadbare with fallibility
patched pants braced up with reason's tangled twine

is sometimes stubborn, says: 'Yet it still moves,'
before the belly tucks in; is shot through
with dark tales we sucked up in childhood's pew
guilt, need, envy and rage, the wailing groves

of never-had and never-was that hang
with offerings in our family trees.
How can thought free in this twilight sees
adrift, widdershins or we ask it be strong

to take on death, eternity, those two
sharp blades that slice poor flesh? Yet we do.

December 1980

Literacy Class

They didn't believe the page would turn easy for them
so they licked a forefinger and took it at the bottom
between damp index and thumb. Look I can still
do it for you. I find myself suddenly
with an ambidextrity I didn't know I had
can take a leaf from high or low.
They had no template of how such things
should be done and it's true the southern corner
doesn't come up simple without a touch of spit.
Opening a book at the top is something
I must have acquired like a way
to say garage almost without noticing.
They were fingering their first own books
the tuppenny novelettes on dried porridge paper
that were folded back on the spine
for easy thrust down cushion side when home
or duty called for reading was a secret vice.
There was no one to show them the holding pattern.
Some pioneer taking up a slim volume
tried to turn where the eye rested at the foot
was all fingers and thumbs but licked
because nothing was done without spit
on the palms for luck or to ward the evil eye
from the tails of white horses, coin and coal brought in
and set a precedent like the one
who bore home knives and forks
angling them on knitting needles rather than pens
to trap their meat without bread.
Now if you were skilled you could
ballet peas on your knife. Do I find it
easier than you who only saw your nannie
do it whereas I was bequeathed it in blood
by my nan. Yet you remembered and I didn't
till you said and I am left to gnaw on other
betrayals I have made and forgotten
in turning the page.

Alma Mater

I have been back today, dinting a way
middle age pilgrims into the late past
of school or college, a quarter century
meeting myself head bent, eyes down, in haste
or my child at just this age it might be
scurrying the corridors. Privileged caste
I know I should think squinched with old envy
my tongue tart with its sweaty steel taste
afraid to round on my cornered image
or see my thin tears fox the half turned page.

I try a name that should be current still.
'A tumour on the brain,' my host says, face
gelling into concern. I fight the chill.
Always one of the lads, your bouncing lass
was the college whore or so went the tale.
Succulent Rita you were succubus
to our dreams. 'And perhaps you can tell
me what Lissauer was like, wrote poetry, was
in the library here?' Tonight I recall
he married a girl from my cousin's school.

'He died last year.' Both older than me
of course but not much, no great divide
of a decade. They stalk my territory
the fens of not-enough-done or even tried.
Promise, that's the true inky Fuseli
beast that squats on the chest, Dracula's bride
who'll leech up heart's blood. Yet I can't see
as the big dipper starts down its last ride
how to get off this track, this Lamia way
that bought my life when it called me out to play.

No good then to kick. The children press by
going somewhere I bless them with. Having none
all become mine though I speak no sermonly
words for them as I should maybe to my own.
Through the common-room window Magritte sky
sewn with staff of life clouds is mannaing down
on river and city planed, the balcony
where we snapped each other almost grown.
Those trees still toss though their leaves black and white
in the shots are grey earth. I am not done, quite.

Cot Death
For a child aged 7 months dead on the last day of January

Terribly the snowdrops pricked today
fresh against the sunned brick wall
in a false Spring that has
blackbird and rook almost building
though all forecasts say
those far humped skybeasts portend
winter still to pall. There's no comfort
in the sun's false heat that steams
from wood and metal a dank breath.

Tonight more natural frost
congeals tears to chill black pearls
time may never dissolve
in the clamped shell of the skull.
There was a bud unclosing
last dark shut forever
will know no summer
no spelling out of fingered shadow
around the sunshine clock
her winter stopped.

Tomorrow's dawn rubs up raw
for her grievers this unhealing sore.

Chattel

Driving back from the literature festival
through Otley handsome in black stone
with white revers of painted windows and doors
I follow behind a tin truck
gaping an open vent high up at the back.
Stopped at the lights the gap is filled
with broad snout, a wet black sponge for sucking up
sweetness from deep in summer grass.
You crane your head in the hole sideways to let
each eye in turn roll up at the sky.
Deep in tumbril shock you don't speak.
I know where you're going this summer's morning
and feel you know it too though how
when no one has ever come back with telltale
smell of blood and fear on staring hide?
I image though I can't see the shrunken dug
flat as a perished rubber glove.
The street is called Wharfedale View. It looks across
to where the moors throw a green quilt
for miles under a high sky. Why can't I just
draw the steel bolt on the tailgate
and let you run and run up there til you drop?
But the lights change. You turn Left; I go Right
for Leeds and perhaps I'm quite wrong
and you're just being moved on to new pasture.
Then why can't I safe home sleep
but see still your face laid along the tailgate
with one moist eye turned up questioning
whether I would have drawn that bolt
if you'd been able to ask me in a tongue
I couldn't kid myself I misunderstood.

Dreaming

Lying awake beside you
that's a white night.
Black nights trudge apart
through treacle tirelessly
blackguarding at every
slung shield changing it
into combat. Here sometimes
an arm or thigh will touch
or your fingers find mine
while I breathe lightly
listening to the come-and-go
tides of your breath.
I am awake to your body's
contour, dear slope and fall
terrain my heart inhabits
outrider from my own dull flesh.

White knight I'd guard
your dreams, fend off
the black bully boy with his
gilt goads to prod you
out of the fields of sleep
so that when you cry
against those white Alps
that freeze, frustrate
I put out my warm hand
in hope to guide you
sweet dreaming home.

Clearing Out

I know this house. I know how the sun
comes lustily in the morning over
the opposite rooftops and won't let you sleep.
I know how orange juice is squeezed out
stickily, the teeth of the glass cone
furring with pitch, not poured from a carton
and tea not made with bags but leaves
that block the waste and are dredged by hand.
I remember the gravyboat with its bilges
brimming with rich silt under a plimsol of fat
a white platelet, carrara veined
you could intaglio with a knife.

I remember waking it seemed unhappily
ever after in this front room where the sun
is busy as a gossipping bourgeoise
about those who lie long and with whom.
I know that on clear days you can see
to Hampstead with the city folded between
a valley I ached to go down into
like any Heidi from these pastures
for dogs, bikes, hybrid teas, pushed mowers
chattering their steel teeth, spanners
on the Sunday pavement, the perverse
underbellies of cars larded wet black.

I know how the steel wool bleeds over the chipped
fingerprints of the drainingboard. Soon
this house will be closed to me forever.
Papers, *The Telegraph* strong on fact and faction
and milk, gold top with a buttered foil of cream
have stopped coming. The silver no longer
demands from the sideboard. Curlicued
EPNS, 'Mother and Dad's wedding present'
will lie heavy at the bottom of a plastic
drawer not hewn, planed, chiselled like the bookcase
they gave you when you went up and girls marched
arm in arm black stockinged to examination
breaking the boys' linked embargo. When I lift
the lid to throw away the tealeaves, ominous
telltales, the dark walls of the dustbin squirm
a live bead fringe charlstoning for a long dead party.

Biographical Fragment: RL 1917—77

So at the last
was it love again
with a girl in a gondola
married seven years before
the muse figureheading
the pointed prow
still above old façades
glazing the waters
with a thin bright skin
a finger could poke through
and dissolve to a cut glass
prism of shifting fragments
each poem a new pattern
of illusion
all done by mirrors
the glittery figments
glimpsed through a hole
bored in the skull
and after, the snap shot
did she trail a hand
in the water, set
the sharp flecks adazzle?

This wasn't at all
like the others: the girls
whose soft arms straight
jacketed you each winter
with an image of renewal
buds sprouting under
their finger tips
Perdita's wreaths
in their childish fair hair.
This one you couldn't put down
last, lost as you let
your hand shatter the surface
and the wild horses
whinny through your head.

Slumped in the taxi
when your heart gave out
you were still carrying
her painted picture, on your way
to have it valued
as if you could ever
put a price on it.
I steal from your quiver
of old tricks. 'Isn't she
beautiful?' you would plead
rapt by her face
the necessary muse

whose eyes always beckon
above the sharp prow
and the broken skin of water
the mermaid you couldn't
live with or without.
'A suicide of wish'
she called it
that death that almost
redeems you, alone
clutching the parcelled
portrait, pretending
you still had somewhere to go.

Mother and the Girl

'Whither thou goest,' she said
thinking: 'Gods but that's a hellhole
desert dry arsehole
no man's land but here would be
an aloneness too stark to suffer
there would be you.'
So she said, elaborating, 'Thy people
will be my people,' meaning
take me into your family
and added as an afterthought
because she knew it would please
her sometime mother-in-law
(does death sever such legal bonds?)
and thy god
shall be my god'
thinking: 'Now what was he called?'

'You sit there a bit
and I'll bring you a cup of goat's milk
or herb tea if you'd rather
but just sit there
and let me wait on you as if
you were still my mother
if only in law.
And Naomi said, 'Yes dear, I will'
because her feet hurt
and anyway Ruth had always been
such a strange girl.
For instance she could never decide
whether she'd really loved her son.
Oh she'd done her duty
looked after him alright.
There was always a hot meal
bubbling in the stewpot when he came in
from the herds and fields, always
a welcome for her not like some
daughters-in-law who won't give
their husband's mother the time
of day. No she couldn't complain:
always the best stool

and the hottest dish and Ruth
asking her if she was comfortable
so that when they died
(Oh my sons) and the other girl
had gone back to her own father
a secondhand pot chipped but
still serviceable, widower's
meat, and they set out for her
old home she had no qualms.
And Ruth organized everything
paying the innkeepers and the porters
getting them camels when the donkeys
ran out. Really she'd been looked after
after just like a queen.
She was going home of course
and the girl hadn't anyone to call
her own. She'd look after her
in Judah and there hadn't been
any need for such speechifying.

So here they were in the land
of milk and honey, only it was Ruth's
all the bees were after as if
they hadn't seen a woman in years.
There was the rich man
kin to Naomi's dead husband
with his goats and vineyards
making his bid and everyone said
'Go on girl; you'll never get
a better offer, a widow and time's
passing.' So she asked, 'What do you think?'
And Naomi said, 'He's a good catch.
Land him,' as if her son had never
been born. Ruth wept a night
and in the morning told him
thinking how the sun
fell through Naomi's hair
and played on her shoulders
and breasts as she splashed
them with water and that
Judah hadn't been that hospitable
they weren't that over the moon

to see her back. 'Listen,'
she said to Boaz. 'Your kinsman's
widow, she's been like a second
mother to me. I couldn't
just walk out and leave her.'
And he looking at her rich
pastures said: 'Fine, bring
the old lady if you want her.'
And Ruth said: 'I do, I do.'

Writers in Residence

Coming to the group each week you have laid
heads, hearts, hands on the line for me to
gun down your choicest dreams, nit pick among
cherished words, bon bons we all unwrap
charily for each other. Coming
to the group each week I have laid too
myself on a line I hoped might be
the shortest distance between our points.
That first day (can you remember?) I was
fearful, probably overloud. So hard
are these things we might never have hit
it off, never made our connection.

One night, I remember, back from spouting
a hit and miss fountain of words somewhere
beyond wintry Newcastle, at the station
the snow barring us from any quick hope
of heading South, I found stranded
voyagers, a community in the bar
so that when the station announcer
called: 'Welcome to Newcastle,' to
travellers that had come through, we
all raising glasses and plastic cups cheered.
That first day, remember, there was
no intermediary. We had to
snowcat out a slippery way
laying our heads, hearts, hands down in trust.

Now I know you all, aspirations
old dreams, have walked savanahs
plains. The smell of the sea enfolds
with the scent of silk and long skirts.
On an eternal Sunday Richard fixes
the generator, children call from a bonfire
dry leaves are swept up for me and flame
so that when we don't meet in flesh
anymore, Saturday afternooning
while the world shops or sports
one of us will remember these lines
laid down, this affair of our hearts
hands, heads that was most like love.

Bullocks

The bullocks have come to stand around us
where we sit after the climb between
the last of summer scabious, Tom Thumb
purple vetch and frilled bladderwrack
of campion flouncing the chalk track.

Hairy hobbledehoys, their coats are soft
still as children's skin. Castrati
who will never come to bullhood
they stare at us mildly. I try to probe
their promptings. Do they want us to speak?

Perhaps it's food they're after: the sacks
of hormone stuffed tasties the husbandman
I use the old word, scatters to keep
their eunuch flesh plump and tender. All boys
together, they have each other in this brief playground.

October's last lush lawn's their lunch counter.
Below, apart, those belles of the swung bag
their mothers brush the browse with tough titties
while the bullfather shoulders his beefcake
waiting alone for his day on, chafing.

Only these gentle lads take notice of us
twolegged interlopers in their workplace
turning out meat and dairy produce
from the green shopfloor. Our dog snaps them back
when curiosity brings them too close in.

Shoulder to shoulder they stand, not jostling.
We're encircled, almost faced down. I can't
look them in their bullseye. That one's galled
biblically. Some have tagged ears, tattoo numbers.
Will they overwinter? My prescience

hangs heavy as the bullish seedpods
or the cows' skin milk jugs. We get to our feet.
Below us the warm house is folded
in a bowl of hills. They stand back as we go
heads turning to snuff our scent, grave bisto kids.

Burning Off

Already autumn stains
a branch here and there
singles out leaves to stopper
their narrow veins with drought
though August's barely out.

Yesterday the yellow combine
tanked through corn
a minotaur carving
its own labyrinth
an iron whopstraw.

A cropped bright stubble
five o'clocks the fields
with stiff gold shafts
one night, then flares
is barbequed black.

Small pointed skulls cremate
slim runners' bones
stripped of sinew crumble
where the smoke stopped them
in their secret track.

These yearly harrowings
libations some god demands
are old as husbandry.
Once it was the delicate seed
of lovers in field or wood.

Now the ground trembles
under a metal stamp muting
the birds' alarm in the broken air.
At night the field is smeared black
under a drained moon.

Morning breaks
in a cold sweat of mist.
The motorway's a distant surf
I launch into. Returning
I drive through a still smutted sunset.

The junctions fall away
at summer's end.
That's where I turned off
in Spring when last year's seed
lay flecked with bonemeal in the ground.

Home again I walk
the unburnt stubble behind my house.
Tomorrow you fly back.
I should pour my heart's blood
out for luck. I do.

Lustre

They kill their lovers mostly
not meaning to of course
no bloody droplet on the pale puffed lobe
in the morning, new pierced
for sleeper with ruby
or snake punctures
full stopping the throat.
That's all old wives' tales.
Their veins flatten with longing.
I see them pare down to a candle shroud.
I know their hot skins, the rouge spots
high up on the cheekbone ridge.

Some seem born prone: orphans
scholars, anyone who plays
the fiddle, strings common speech
into verse, battening it down with rhyme
or is too drawn to dancing.
It's in their blood you might say
or runs where the marrow should be
bone deep, sipped in with mother's milk.
I blame above all those dreaming nurses
whose goneaway eyes charge their soft breasts
with junket curds and thin blue whey.

They don't come to me of course
aren't joined by my hands
but elsewhere they say
bringing their brides home.
I know at once meeting them
at the pump by the sly downcast look
and their beauty. I know too
when a girl comes back to die
and the old wives chatter of lover
or husband gone that when I call
with comfort and chrism her gaze
will walk beyond me through the kneehigh
window, the cheap ring twist
loose knuckling the finger, unwedlocked.

I try to warn them on Sundays
while the motes sift down
a sand sermon trickling between
dead men's crabbed fingers.
I can see from my pulpit stare
the eyes already too bright
fern-seeded against the visible world
of warm flesh and blood. Their hearts
lie like virgins waiting.
Those others have only to beckon.

They never stay of course, having always
somewhere else to be, a mirrorskip
of air or water, woods or the black bowels
of hills where their other lovers wait.
When I hear of a drowning I know
one of them has gone home. I take
my hat and great cape out into the rain
knock on the shut door to read the burial
service over the living and their mortal wound.

The love of good men and women can save
sometimes, humdrum days, progeny
churning milk, turning the earth.
They must be fetched back from those fields
where they pluck starshine out of night's furrows.
I can tell them how, those who would go
about it, that they must hold on
however the loved shape changes
or shrill cries surround them, carry away
the still form that hangs like dead.

They will hanker at first, or forever
for those lovers they couldn't hold
but who never let them go. Upstairs
my wife sits at the window watching
for a shape to step out of the trees
detach its dress from the rags of leaves
the wind puckers. It's my time
to call her and the children, to see
her finger trace the glazed purple bruise
rimming the eye of each cup before
she lets fall the dark brackish stream
that is our daily infusion.

Prague Letter

We are here on embassy.
Fair Helen or Eleanor
'You can translate it how you wish,'
greets us downstairs from the Ministry of Culture
attendant spirit in this masque of winter
gives us our crowns to spend
and our programme, strides a lithe Artemis
in her blue autumn coat, booty of an old trip
to Peter Jones, out into the dazed morning.
We are in Bohemia.

       *

You were hard to come at: the airport
socked in with fog sent us south to Budapest.
Below on the tarmac the bowser driver
gobs broad Magyar faced at the plane wheel
before coupling up. A boy moustached
operetta handsome in sludge green
yawns easing his Kalashnikov. We must
go back by coach. We queue for fresh papers.
Our road follows the black Danube.
At the new border another boy with franking set
slung round his neck like an old clippie
sets his mark on our passports.

       *

Eighty one years ago you were born
Armenian. 'I am never going out. I lost all
my wife, my partner,' The deaf aid won't transmit
their claims that you have no visa.
We plead that you become our scapegoat
to bureaucracy and let us go on
to where your young sister waits with her hands full
of seventy four years. Spry still you go down
the iron steps. They pat your shoulder as we drive away.
The fog comes out to meet us beyond Bratislava
a name I conjure back from some bulletin
half heard on the rug in front of the fire
calling up distant guns to Sunday tea.

       *

Three hundred years since we failed you
pinching the privy purse; sent you a princess
but no money. Thirty year war ripped Europe.
I am here on embassy. The grave students
follow my foreign tongue as I try to sketch
white flowers in the chalky air.
The winter city queens beside the Vlata
powdering her hair with fine dry snow.
'Good evening. This is the operator.
In England there is no answer.'

                    *

Under our feet the dead are stacked ten deep.
The headstones stumble in the broken earth
tilt their testament script, stagger
between the acacias that let fall
their small grey drops of leaves.
Here and there a single dice of cobble
is placed in tribute. These are old dead.
Katka's elsewhere beyond the ghetto stones.
We do not go into the house that holds
the names of all who died, preferring
the archives of neat silver and stitches
monuments to the living fingers
that chased or bound these trappings
in synagogue furniture
til the wall came down, an intimacy
relearned later in truck and windowless chamber.

                    *

'What do they think,' we ask fair Helen
'the parties of tourists whose fathers
stamped the transit papers, kept the files?'
We climb up to the kingless castle
he could almost see from his dwarf house
in Alchemist's Street as he transmitted
lead into golden words, a coffin room
a cell he filled with honey of despair.
I post my letter to Milena.
'In England there is no answer.'

                    *

292

Exiled Elizabeth came home, kept court.
Katka coughed up his lungs in Vienna. The trucks rolled.
This is an embassy, a little exile
by favour of the British Council. We smile
and translate our thoughts into homely pidgin.
Each morning we shake hands with our hosts
as if meeting for the first time, after
the custom of Bohemia, and everywhere
except taut England. Yet in the streets
asking the way I get the greeting
'You are English? Before the war my grandmother
went twice a year in March and June to London.
Take the Right; no, no, I mean the Left.'

*

'They want to live. They don't want to make
politics. I am a cosmopolitan.' Pissed
before take-off, you raise your double
burden into the sky high. Survivor
your skin is parchment tight, your bones are ash.
The passengers turn away as you amble
towards them tottering like your gravestone
gallant still as a way to put down death.
'Sit here,' you plead, patting the seat beside you.
Last night of my exile the words fell like rain
on these fields parched they tell us six months.
'This is the operator. I have England for you.'

Remembering

'I forget dear,' you used to say. 'Ask Pa.
He'll know.' Today, your birthday it was me
forgot, knowing you wouldn't remember, far
away from time. Shadows are what you see

they come to take the things you hide
and forget, or out of the past will be home
when the pubs close so you wait up, wide
awake for dead footsteps, never quite alone.

You aren't yourself, although you go still
in that fleshly dress we recognize and love
and somewhere inside is the girl with bicycle
I have in my album of photographs, but move

through twilight like those sepia prints: you
in a wide-brimmed hat for christening or there
strolling the pier with your only lover, two
of a kindness that never looked elsewhere.

Now you trust he will be waiting for you, and I
who can't believe, must pray you go down on a lie.

Preserves

Only the rich ate marmalade. We had red jam
that soaked through the grey bread like blood on lint.
It might have been the war we always blamed
for everything but yet inside I knew it wasn't.

Once visiting a schoolfriend, doctor's daughter
staying the night strangely in a strange house, I looked
for it at breakfast but was only offered
honey, gilt beespit to spread on leisured toast.

This Wednesday for the first time I really made it
in your country kitchen, scalded, skinned and sliced
added white drifts of sweetness to bitter fruit
and simmered til the peel was clear as the ice

we'd played with childishly that afternoon
duck and draking the jagged panes to smithereens
on the pond's skating surface, a brittle moon
you wanted to crack. The pots gleam golden

with candied slivers aswim in a sharp sauce.
Filled with you I know I'm rich too, at last.

Doing the Flowers

Unbelieving I follow you into the chill twilight
of the nave, beached boat on the chalk waves of the downs.
There's pulpit and altar to be garlanded in a rite
older than a Roman cross. We deadhead among the bouquets
garnis for service. I track down the mysteries
of dustpan and brush, pail we take to the tap
for living water. Back in the vestry boot cupboard
I feel no blasphemy against my god
who lets his arrow still transfix me or his mother
demanding my homage. On Sunday you will kneel
and not see my hand in the pulpit fringe of flowers
or hear my voice raising our psalm while apart
serving my bitter bread and sour wine I long
for the conversion of lip to lip. I lift
the dusty curtain over the door into daylight.
Outside the hard mouths of the long dead cry that only love
can make conjunctions of the indifferent stars.

Seasons
for T and A V

Yesterday they were separated. All night
lambs' long thin baas have woven with ewes'
deep piled lows a mat of grieving over late
summer fields slubbed with drought's succulent dews.

Martins hammer at the eaves still. The swifts
have sailed for Egypt and sickle swallows home
away. Trunks are packed; new gym shoes etch sharp prints.
Fresh cut ridges lie marled with sour pig dung

for the plough's knife. The sheep fall silent then let
a bitter reprise loose in the milk rinsed dawn
for the rubbery snuggle of lips and teat.
The ewes' bellies will swell with those to be born.
Autumn sounds a new sprung stave for them to learn
but the lambs' fate is tabled. Some things never return.

Epitaphs From West Brompton

'The public are permitted to walk in the cemetery daily.
There is no thoroughfare.'

The squirrel flirts his feather duster
among the everlasting sweetpeas
a crochet of pink and mauve vulvas
slung between the grey bedheads.
I follow him, cribbling tales from the slabbed texts
foxed into obscurity by time and weather.

*

This stone house holds *a devoted*
gentle son; elder and dutiful, born in Japan
died in Colombo at twenty-two. Exhumed a year later
he was brought home on his almost birthday in Spring.
His mother set this cameo high Tom Brown collared
above the temple door where she could
worship each week with flowers while
her grief wheeled over the cracked plain
her young caesar fell on fevered.

*

Doris, Florrie, Eliza, Minnie
daughters, wives, all beloved.
Here death fruits the blackberry
from its white maiden flower.

*

War booted this boy from his founding father's feet.
He tackled and scored across the aery pitch
until the away team's guns bucked
the leather helmeted head from his shoulders.
Dad drummed up boys to fill his place.
I saw today those inheritors
of the sky's blues ganging outside the gate
for training. Father and son lie crumbled
in each other's arms while the crowds
still roar on their terraces.

*

Ardent Moffrey, suddenly called away
his sharp flame snuffed by the wind's blue pinch.

*

Here's a common iconography
of draped urn, severed hands linked
mourning angel as young woman, hand raised
in blessing or hope, stone gaze downcast
hair furrowed in Amami waves by Burne Jones.
Here's commonwealth: son Christopher died
in Kiwi Pakeraire; Sir John governed
pumiced Fiji while the pigmy head
on his watchain was stopped at ten to two.
As the century turned, an Irishman
was cut down in pigtailed Swatow
and died dreaming of soft Armagh.
Yet they couldn't lie still. They must come home.
The brass handled chests of tropic bone
or desert mummy were shipped back stowage
not wanted on the voyage while the live
leant on the beaded rail above, flirting
under a sick moon that had crossed her datelines.

*

Let us celebrate the Love family.
Incestuous blendings they are folded
together, siblings meet and meat
in their detached residence, grave couplings
they beat back with maidenhair fern
and shroud antimaccasser, lazily
circling wings trapped at last
on the buzzing flypaper, held fast
til death inked them indelibly
into the long scroll that holds their legend
yoked under father's name.

*

On the Fitch vault Dave and Fern proclaim
'they aren't dead yet. Ha, ha!' in letters of soot.

*

299

John Peake, Knight, sent the wheels
marrying the bucket and spade, briefcase
Betjemanian Brighton and Southcoast line
threaded with grazing cows on a green ground.
Under the banking smoke of pigeon wings
he dipped his pen and the trains ran on time.

                    *

Some are calcified snatching at eternity
in sailor suit or hair ribbon the breeze can't stir.
Champion sculler of Tyne and Thames leans
on stone oars while marrow airship
striped with lichen and brittle wasp fighter
are raised from the smooth hard sky by public
subscription. Black marble fruit
giant's grapeshop press the general's
shoulderblades into the earth, old blood
stained with rusty coin of his medals.

                    *

Forty years of pensioners come home
to die in peace lie anonymous
under their common memorial, bonemeal
having fought for Queen, England, Empire
surrounded by the teenagers of the trenches
with Tom Foy, comedian, Emmeline
Pankhurst, wife, and Percy who tried
to outrun time at Brooklands
first at a hundred miles in an hour
that caught him up.

                    *

On sunny afternoons at closing time
the lusty come to fondle among the unblinking
watchers, lie on their hard beds, drop seed
in the rancid earth, resurrect
between the dank bungalows, knowing
how the gates clang to at sundown
when the squirrel and the slow weeds inherit.

                    *

We are only allowed to walk in the cemetery
daily. There is no thoroughfare.

300

Encounter

Up the lane Horus has parked on a post
so still he seems carved, a totem not
warm flesh and feather. His head's a wedge
holding grey flannel sky and sludge earth apart.

No light bringer; the tenement hedge
is silent but breaks into tumult
as I trudge up behind the dog's neat paws
scoring pock marks in the damp chalk.

Hawk blinks once quick over the sickle beak and claws
shutting us out. The dun sparrows panic
stepped up in the highrise blackthorn flapping
whether to mob him or flee. Mesmeric

he's yet as out of place in the lane capping
the familiar pole as death is everywhere.
How could the Nile punters see sun in him whose feet
tear the sky to tatters with the small birds fear?

Dog and I turn back. Could he snatch her, meat
hooks in her spine, legs kicking against cloud foam
eyriewards? But he's gone. The lane unfurls.
Sparrows take up their gossip and we are coming home.